FRANÇOIS R — P9-BIQ-954

Gargantua
and
Pantagruel

SELECTIONS

TRANSLATED AND EDITED BY
Floyd Gray
UNIVERSITY OF MICHIGAN

Crofts Classics

GENERAL EDITORS

Samuel H. Beer, *Harvard University*
O. B. Hardison, Jr., *The Folger Shakespeare Library*

AHM Publishing Corporation
Arlington Heights, Illinois 60004

ISBN: 0-88295-068-1
(Formerly 390-23295-5)

Library of Congress Card Number: 66-12976

PRINTED IN THE UNITED STATES OF AMERICA
757
Seventh Printing

CONTENTS

THE SECOND BOOK—PANTAGRUEL

CONTENTS

INTRODUCTION

François Rabelais (c.1494-c.1553), the son of a prosperous lawyer, was born near the town of Chinon in the province of Touraine. Practically nothing is known of his early years. We do know, however, from a letter which he penned to Guillaume Budé, the greatest Hellenist of the day, that in 1521 he was already a Franciscan friar and a student of Greek. His studies were looked upon with suspicion by his fellow monks who prided themselves on their simple piety, and Rabelais decided to transfer to the more sympathetic rule of the learned Benedictines. Sometime before 1530 he gave up monastic life altogether, went to Paris for a while, and finally registered as a medical student at the University of Montpellier. On November 1, 1532, he was appointed physician to the Hospital at Lyons, and on the last day of the same month, we find him writing a remarkable Latin letter to Erasmus in which he expresses his filial devotion, and the debt which he owes to his writings. During the course of the same year, Rabelais published in Lyons, under the pseudonym of Alcofribas Nasier, his *Pantagruel, King of the Dipsodes.*

Following a journey to Rome as medical attendant and secretary to Cardinal du Bellay, one of the great political churchmen of the day, Rabelais returned to Lyons and published in 1534 his *Most Horrific Life of the Great Gargantua, Father of Pantagruel.* The *Third Book of Pantagruel,* published in 1546, was the first to appear under Rabelais's own name. It was condemned at once by the Sorbonne, and Rabelais was obliged to flee to the safety of the Imperial city of Metz. In 1552, exactly twenty years after the first book, Rabelais published the *Fourth Book of Pantagruel.* The facts surrounding his last years and death are as obscure and uncertain as those of his birth and early years. There is reason to believe that he died in Paris, probably in 1553. The posthumous *Fifth Book,* which appeared in 1564, is of doubtful authenticity; it was most probably compiled by some unknown person who had access to Rabelais's notes and manuscripts.

Pantagruel and *Gargantua* deal with the birth, genealogy, childhood, education, and deeds of their respective
giants. They are constructed, therefore, according to the
same fairly uncomplicated narrative line as the epic poems
and chivalric novels they are meant to parody. The struc-
ture of the *Third Book*, on the other hand, is quite unlike
anything the world of fiction had ever seen. It does not
present the life and exploits of a hero, nor the resolution
of a complicated situation; its line of development is cir-
cular rather than chronological. Panurge has become the
center of interest, and the book he dominates follows a
fictional line drawn and erased countless times; it is elab-
orated about a theme and variations, a single question with
countless answers. To marry or not to marry, Panurge asks
himself and a host of improbable characters. Unable to
obtain a satisfactorily unambiguous reply, he decides to
consult the oracle of the Holy Bottle. The *Fourth Book*
deals with the voyage and adventures of Panurge and his
merry crew. Their odyssey takes them from one fantastic
island to another, plunges them into a violent and almost
fatal storm, and leaves them at the end of the book still
far short of their eventual destination. The *Fifth Book*
contains the continuation of the journey and the conclusion
to the quest, the sanctuary of the Holy Bottle. Its long
awaited pronouncement consists of a single word: drink!
Neither Panurge nor the reader is immediately certain of
the symbolic meaning of this injunction, and subsequent
commentators have interpreted it in a number of ways.
But Rabelais seems to be saying—and his words recall
those the Delphic oracle spoke to Socrates—that self-
knowledge is to be found within, that to know oneself is
to live fully and deeply.

Within this relatively uncomplicated narrative frame-
work, Rabelais has permitted his exuberant fancy and
imagination to run wild. The reader is overwhelmed in a
torrent of words, is confronted with what is perhaps the
greatest example of comic verbalization in all literature.
In Rabelais's hands the word becomes flesh, creates a
world, peoples it with strange creatures, plants it with a
fantastic variety of trees, herbs, and flowers, fills it with
libraries of books in several languages, forms a universe
sufficiently disorienting and complex to sustain the pres-

ence of a giant. An astonishing manipulator of linguistic technique, Rabelais is as capable as James Joyce of abrupt variations of style, of parody, of strange, mysterious landscapes and figures, of drunken laughter. The good Doctor claims therapeutic value for his works, prescribes them as an unfailing tonic against the toil, trouble, and tears of life. Laughter, he reminds us after Aristotle, is natural to man.

But Rabelais's book is violent, raging, tortured underneath its laughter; it is realistic in its reflection of the unsettling clash, the deluge of new and strange discoveries, the whirlwind of contradictory theories and opinions with which man of the early Renaissance was buffeted. The chapters on the birth, childhood, education of Gargantua and Pantagruel are also a satire on the ills of the society of the day. The Abbey of Thélème—which grows and takes shape, much as Plato's Republic, before our very eyes—is Rabelais's myth of some future Utopia. The *Third Book* derives much of its comic material from antifeminist literature and attitudes; but the labyrinth of doubt and contradiction which Panurge insists upon constructing about himself anticipates the philosophical skepticism of Montaigne's *Apology of Raimond Sebond*. The *Fourth Book* transports us to an archipelago of strange islands inhabited by characters as hallucinatory as those which haunt the paintings of Breughel. Allegorical in the main, these figures are vast anatomizations of Fear, Lent, Lust, Gluttony. Having examined the follies of man in his earlier volumes, Rabelais now reviews and catalogues his vices.

One of the most significant things about Rabelais's work is its ambiguity. It has been considered an elaborate allegory, a political or personal satire, a pamphlet against Catholicism, a manifesto of atheism, a repository of hidden knowledge. The great French critic Sainte-Beuve has described it as a mixture of science, obscenity, comedy, eloquence, and high fantasy, that suggests everything yet is comparable to nothing, that seizes you and disconcerts you, intoxicates and disgusts you, and about which—after having vastly enjoyed and admired it—you may still ask yourself seriously whether or not you understood it. If Rabelais has been interpreted and misinterpreted so consistently, if he has been subjected to constant and systematic exegesis, it is in great part because his book affords no single point of view and no unqualified conclusions. Although the universe it posits is generally recognized as a compound of the fantastic and the realistic, interpreters have on the whole based their views on the realistic and satiric element and dismissed, or better subsumed, the fantastic aspect as simply the mode appropriate to comedy, the vehicle by which the satirical message is conveyed. By this approach the author's point of view becomes an essentially critical one, with reformative overtones, and his work turns into an explicit commentary on the daily social, political, religious, and economic life of the France of the day. Such commentary is, of course, present, but if the whole work is made to exist to serve this point, then there is a strange dichotomy between form and function. Rabelaisian reality is comprised of disparate and frequently contradictory elements—it is never a mirror of life, but a metaphor.

The universe that comes from Rabelais's pen contains the ingredients of an *Iliad*, an *Odyssey*, a *Divine* and a *Human Comedy*. It is as encyclopedic and composite, as complex and chaotic as the age it represents. Man of the Renaissance, Rabelais has produced the novel of the Renaissance. He has captured in his pages the aspirations, hesitations, turmoil, and enthusiasm of a century in the throes of radical change. Throughout his book, Rabelais is the apostle of moderation, and a critic of excesses of every kind. He terms his philosophy Pantagruelism, and he defines it as an attitude implying joyous acceptance of the things of life together with a full consciousness of their vanity. If we accept Rabelais's book as he himself offers it, that is, as a substantial draught from his creative barrel, then we will be able to appreciate its multiple aspects and its various perspectives, to view it essentially as a world where words change and grow, reel in drunken exuberance, exist in constant movement and metamorphosis.

A translator is faced with many problems—especially a translator of Rabelais. So much that is characteristic of his genius depends upon verbal creation and semantic confusion that a translation can be little more than an approximation. Sir Thomas Urquhart and Peter Motteux,

Rabelais's seventeenth-century translators, were eminently successful in capturing the tone and texture of the original; but their version is a veritable re-creation, a brilliant re-casting and expansion rather than a faithful translation. More recent translators, such as Samuel Putnam (*All the Extant Works of François Rabelais,* New York, 1929), Jacques Leclerc (*The Complete Works of Rabelais,* New York, The Modern Library, 1944), and J. M. Cohen (*The Histories of Gargantua and Pantagruel,* Penguin Books, 1955), adhere more closely to the text, but Leclerc interlards it with parenthetical explanations and Putnam and Cohen are frequently archaic in language as well as in syntax. In making my own translation, I have been concerned first and foremost with providing an accurate, literal, readable version in modern American English. I have not hesitated to use, however, whenever Rabelais has done so, a simple or a complex expression, a pompous or a facetious tone, a pedantic or an obscene word, a periodic or an elliptic construction. I have included in my translation substantial portions of *Pantagruel* and *Gargantua* as well as some of the most significant chapters of the *Third Book* and the *Fourth Book.* I have decided to eliminate the *Fifth Book* entirely for reasons of space; it seemed preferable in a volume of this size to give selections only from those parts of the work which are incontestably authentic. I have made every effort to preserve some kind of narrative continuity throughout, and this intention accounts for the regrettable but unavoidable omission of certain familiar chapters and episodes. My translation is based on the text and commentary of Jacques Boulenger and Lucien Scheler's one-volume edition (*Oeuvres complètes,* Paris, Bibliothèque de la Pléiade, 1959) and on Marcel Guilbaud's elegant five-volume edition (*Oeuvres complètes,* Paris, Imprimerie Nationale, 1957). I have consulted as well the critical—and still incomplete—edition begun by Abel Lefranc (*Oeuvres de François Rabelais,* Paris, Champion, 1912-31, vols. I-V; Genève, Droz, 1955, vol. VI) for help in translating difficult and obscure passages. It is hoped that the present translation—in spite of the fact that it is only a partial one—will provide the reader with some idea of the magnificent depth and extraordinary sweep of the complete work.

PRINCIPAL DATES
IN THE LIFE OF RABELAIS

1494   Probable date of Rabelais's birth. According to a well-founded tradition, he was born at La Devinière, a family property not far from Chinon.

c.1511   Entered the Franciscan Monastery at Fontenay-le-Comte.

c.1525   Persecuted for his study of Greek, Rabelais obtained papal authorization to transfer from the Franciscans to the Benedictine monastery at Maillezais.

1530   Registered at the University of Montpellier on September 17 and received his Bachelor of Medicine November 1.

1532   Appointed doctor at the Hospital of Lyons. Publication of *Pantagruel*.

1534   Publication of *Gargantua*.

1536   Received papal absolution for having left his monastery in 1530.

1537   Rabelais is awarded his Doctorate of Medicine at Montpellier.

1546   Publication of the *Third Book*.

1548   Partial publication in Lyons of the *Fourth Book*.

1552   Publication in Paris of the *Fourth Book*.

1553   Probable date of Rabelais's death.

1562   Posthumous publication of first sixteen chapters of the *Fifth Book*.

1564   Publication of the entire *Fifth Book*.

THE FIRST BOOK

The Most Horrific Life of the Great Gargantua Father of Pantagruel [1]

COMPOSED IN DAYS OF OLD
BY MASTER ALCOFRIBAS [2]
ABSTRACTOR OF QUINTESSENCE
BOOK FULL OF PANTAGRUELISM [3]

TO THE READERS

O friendly readers who peruse this book,
Divest yourselves now of every passion,
And pray be not scandalized as you look,
For it contains no evil or infection.
It is true that very little perfection,
Except in laughter you will sight;
Yet in nothing else can my heart delight,
When I view the sorrow of your brief span.
It is better of laughter than of tears to write,
Because laughter is natural to man.

THE AUTHOR'S PROLOGUE

Most illustrious drinkers, and you, most precious syphilitics—because to you, and to no others, my writings are dedicated—Alcibiades, in Plato's dialogue entitled the

---

[1] Although *Gargantua* (1534) was composed after *Pantagruel* (1532), it is the first book in the series since it deals with the life of Pantagruel's father [2] **Alcofribas** is Rabelais's anagram. Our author adopted a pseudonym because, as a Humanist, he might not have wanted to sign his name to a work that was not in Latin, especially one which he was publishing without a royal privilege, and one which could prove dangerous for him [3] **Pantagruelism** is the name Rabelais gives the "philosophy" of his books

Symposium, praising his preceptor Socrates (without question the prince of philosophers), says, among other things, that he is similar to the Sileni. Sileni, in days gone by, were little boxes, like the ones we now see in apothecaries' shops with joyful and frivolous figures painted on them, such as harpies, satyrs, trussed birds, horned hares, saddled ducks, flying goats, harnessed deer, and other pictures of the same kind designed expressly to incite people to laugh (for such was Silenus,[1] master of the good Bacchus); but on the inside were preserved fine drugs such as balm, ambergris, amomum,[2] musk and civet,[3] medicinal stones and other precious things. Now this is the way Alcibiades said Socrates was,[4] because, seeing him from the outside and judging him by his external appearance, you would not have given an onion peel for him so ugly he was of body and so ridiculous of aspect, with a pointed nose, the stare of a bull, the face of a fool, simple in manners, rustic in clothing, poor in fortune, unfortunate in women, unfit for all public duties, always laughing, always drinking as much as anybody and everybody, always demeaning himself, always dissimulating his divine wisdom; but, upon opening the box, you would have found within a celestial and priceless drug: a more than human understanding, marvelous virtues, invincible courage, an unparalleled sobriety, complete contentment, perfect assurance, incredible contempt for all those things for which men lie awake, run about, labor, sail, and fight.

What is the purpose, in your opinion, of this prelude and beginning? It is because you, my good disciples, and certain other idle fools, reading the joyful titles of some of our books, such as *Gargantua, Pantagruel, Downbottle, The Dignity of Codpieces, Peas and Bacon cum commento,* etc.,[5] assume too hastily that there is to be found nothing

[1] **Silenus** is the foster father and teacher of Bacchus as well as the leader of the satyrs   [2] **amomum** an aromatic shrub   [3] **civet** a substance secreted by the civet cat, used in perfumery   [4] **Socrates** this comparison, a favorite among Humanists of the time, was popularized by one of the *Adages* of Erasmus   [5] **Gargantua . . . commento** the first two titles only are by Rabelais; the other three are fictitious and facetious—*cum commento:* with a commentary, a medieval gloss

inside except mockeries, frivolities, and joyful prevarications since the sign hung outside (the title, that is), without further investigation, is commonly received with derision and guffaw. But it is not appropriate to appraise the works of men with such levity. You yourself say that the habit does not make the monk, and a person can be dressed in a monk's habit who, inside, is anything but a monk, and a person can wear a Spanish cape who, insofar as courage is concerned, has nothing to do with Spain. This is why you must open the book and carefully weigh its contents. Then you will realize that the drug contained within is definitely of another value than the box would lead one to suppose, that is to say that the subjects treated here are not so frivolous as the title on the outside would indicate.

And supposing that you do find matter that is quite amusing and which corresponds fully to the title, you should not stop there, however, as if it were the Siren's song,[6] but you should interpret in a higher sense what, by chance, you may think was said in a lighthearted way.

Have you never opened any bottles? Son of a bitch! Remember the expression you had. Or have you never seen a dog coming upon a marrow-bone? He is, as Plato says, *lib. II de Rep.*,[7] the most philosophic beast in the world. If you have seen one, you certainly noticed with what devotion he looks at it, with what care he guards it, with what fervor he holds it, with what prudence he bites into it, with what affection he breaks it, and with what diligence he sucks it. What induces him to do this? What does he expect from his effort? What does he hope to gain? Nothing more than a little marrow. It is true that this little is more delicious than a lot of many other kinds of nourishment because marrow is a food which nature has worked out to perfection, as Galen states *iii Facu. natural.*[8] and *xi, De usu parti.*[9]

[6] **Siren's song** according to Greek legend was so sweet that sailors were hypnotized by it   [7] *lib. II de Rep.* Book II, Plato's *Republic.* Rabelais's abbreviations were understandable to Humanists   [8] *Facu. natural. On the Natural Faculties*   [9] *De usu parti. On the Uses of the Parts of the Body of Man.*

Following the dog's example, you should be wise, sniffing, smelling and evaluating these fine and meaty books, swift in the pursuit and bold in the attack. Then, by careful reading and frequent meditation, you should break open the bone and suck the substantific marrow—that is to say, the meaning of the Pythagorean symbols which I use—in the certain hope of becoming prudent and valorous from such a reading. In doing this, you will find quite a different taste, and a more abstruse doctrine which will reveal to you high sacraments and horrific mysteries not only about our religion, but also our political state and economic life.

Do you honestly believe that Homer, writing the *Iliad* and *Odyssey,* ever thought about the allegories which Plutarch, Heracleides Ponticus, Eustathius, and Phornutus[10] have stuffed into them, and which Politian[11] has pilfered from them? If you believe it, you do not come within a hand or a foot of my opinion which is that Homer thought of them about as much as Ovid thought of the sacraments of the Gospel in writing his *Metamorphoses.* Yet Friar Simple, a real sponger if ever there was one, took it upon himself to point them out to anyone as foolish as he he came across, or, whenever he met, as the proverb says, a lid for such a pot.[12]

If you do not believe it, what reason is there for believing it of these new and joyful chronicles, seeing that, in dictating them, I thought no more about it than you did, you who were perhaps drinking like myself? For in the composition of this masterly book, I did not waste nor spend any more, nor any other time than that allotted for my bodily refection, that is to say for eating and drinking. This is precisely the time for writing about these high matters and deep sciences, as Homer, paragon of all philologists, was well aware, and Ennius, father of the Latin

[10] **Plutarch . . . Phornutus** authors, or as in the case of Plutarch, supposed authors of commentaries on Homer   [11] **Politian** Italian humanist (15th cen.), author of an *Eulogy of Homer*   [12] **a lid for such a pot** the right type of person to listen to such nonsense

poets, so Horace claims, even though some lout has said that his poetry smelled more of wine than of oil.

A rascal has said as much of my books; but a turd to him! The odor of wine, oh how much more delicate, pleasing, compelling, more celestial and delicious than that of oil! And I shall be as proud to have it said of me that I have spent more on wine than on oil as Demosthenes was when it was said of him that he spent more on oil than on wine. I find only honor and glory in being called and considered a good fellow and a good companion—and with this name I am welcome in any good company of Pantagruelists.[13] Demosthenes was reproached by a sourpuss who said that his *Orations* smelled like the apron of a foul and filthy oil merchant. Interpret, however, all my doing and sayings in the very best light; hold in reverence the cheese-shaped brain which feeds you this fine nonsense and, to the best of your ability, think of me as always joyous.

Now, my hearties, enjoy yourselves, and gaily read the rest for the contentment of your bodies and the profit of your kidneys! But listen, ass-heads (may a chancre lame you!), remember to drink to my health, and I promise to do the same at once.

On the Genealogy and Antiquity of Gargantua

I refer you to the *Great Pantagrueline Chronicle*[1] for an idea of the genealogy and antiquity from which Gargantua descended. Here you will learn in greater detail how giants were born in this world, and how, from them, in direct line, sprang Gargantua, father of Pantagruel. And you will not be angry if for today I go on—although the topic is such that the more it is recalled, the more it pleases your Lordships, as Plato asserts in his *Philebo* and *Gorgias*, and Flaccus,[2] who says that there are certain subjects (ours is

[13] **Pantagruelists** followers of Pantagruelism   [1] ***Great . . . Chronicle*** allusion to *Pantagruel,* published in 1532   [2] **Flaccus** Horace, Roman poet

one, no doubt) which become more delectable the more they are repeated.

Would to God that every one were as certain about his genealogy from Noah's ark down to the present day! I think that there are many now who are emperors, kings, dukes, princes, and popes who are descended from relic and hod carriers, just as, contrariwise, many are almhouse beggars, needy and miserable, who are descended in blood and line from great kings and emperors as a result of the marvelous handing down of realms and empires:

> From the Assyrians to the Medes,
> From the Medes to the Persians,
> From the Persians to the Macedonians,
> From the Macedonians to the Romans,
> From the Romans to the Greeks,
> From the Greeks to the French.

And to give you an idea of the person who is talking to you, I believe that I am descended from some rich king or prince of yesteryear; for you never saw a man who had a greater desire to be king and rich than I, so as to be able to live and eat well, not to have to work, no to have to worry, to enrich my friends and all men of good will and wisdom. But in this thought I find comfort, that in the other world I shall be even greater than I dare to hope now. With such or with a better thought, enliven your unhappiness and drink hearty, if you can.

Coming back to our sheep, I was telling you that the antiquity and genealogy of Gargantua were preserved for us by a sovereign gift of heaven more completely than any other, except for the Messiah's. I'll not talk about this, for it's none of my business, and, besides, the devils (that is, the slanderers and hypocrites) are against it. And it was found by Jean Audeau[3] in a meadow that he owned near the Gualeau Arch, below a farm called The Olive, on the road to Narsay.[4] Dredging in this meadow, the diggers

---

[3] **Andeau** probably someone Rabelais actually knew   [4] **Gualeau Arch . . . Narsay** actual localities near Rabelais' birthplace

struck a great bronze tomb with their picks, immeasurably long—they never did find the end of it because it went too far into the sluices of the Vienne.[5] Opening the tomb where it was marked with a goblet, around which was written, in Etruscan letters, *HIC BIBITUR,*[6] they found nine flagons set up in the same way as they set up ninepins in Gascony.[7] The middle one turned out to be a great, greasy, grand, grey, pretty, little, mouldy booklet, stronger, but not sweeter smelling than roses.

In this was found the said genealogy, written out at length in chancellery letters,[8] not on paper, not on parchment, not on wax, but on a piece of elm bark so worn with age, however, that you could hardly read three of them in a row.

I (although unworthy) was summoned, and with a great strain of spectacles, putting to use the art, as taught by Aristotle, by which one can read invisible letters, I translated it, as you will see in your pantagruelizing—that is to say, in drinking your fill and reading about the horrific exploits of Pantagruel.

At the end of the book was a short treatise entitled: *The Antidoted Baubles.*[9] Rats and roaches or (to be exact) some other evil beasts had nibbled away the beginning. I have copied the rest of it below, out of respect for antiquity.

How Gargantua was Carried Eleven Months in his Mother's Belly

Grandgousier was a good fellow in his day. He liked to drink his fill as much as any man in the world, and he liked to eat salty food. He usually had for this purpose a good supply of Mayence and Bayonne hams, a great lot of smoked beef tongue, an abundance of chitterlings[1] in sea-

---

[5] **Vienne** river which flows through Chinon [6] *Hic Bibitur* Drink here [7] **as they . . . Gascony** in rows of three [8] **chancellery letters** in the cursive hand of the Papal Chancellery [9] *The . . . Baubles* is a verse composition of which no one yet has ever been able to make sense [1] **chitterlings** the small intestines of pigs

son and salted beef with mustard, a store of fish-eggs, plenty of sausages, and not from Bologna (for he was afraid of Lombard poison)[2] but from Bigorre, from Langaulnay, from Brenne, and from Rouergue.[3]

Having attained manhood, he married Gargamelle, daughter of the King of the Butterflies, a pretty wench with a good mug on her. Together they often played the two-backed beast, blissfully rubbing their blubber together until Gargamelle became pregnant with a fine son. And she carried him for eleven months.

For women can be pregnant that long, even longer, especially when it is some masterpiece of a person who is to perform great feats in his lifetime. Homer tells us that the child which Neptune engendered with a nymph was born a full year later—in the twelfth month, that is. For (as A. Gellius, *lib. III*[4] says) this long time was in keeping with Neptune's majesty, and it assured that the child would be formed to perfection. By the same token, Jupiter made the night that he slept with Alcmena last forty-eight hours, for in less time he would not have been able to forge Hercules who purged the world of monsters and tyrants.

The gentlemen Pantagruelists of antiquity have confirmed what I say, and have declared not only possible, but legitimate as well, the child born of a woman in the eleventh month after her husband's death:

Hippocrates, *lib. De alimento*,

Pliny, *li. XVI, cap. v*,

Plautus, *in Cistellaria*,

Marcus Varro, in the satire entitled *The Testament*, quotes Aristotle to this effect,

Censorinus, *li. De die natali*,

Aristotle, *libr. VII, capi. iii et iv, de nat. animalium*,

[2] **Lombard poison** the Italians were notorious poisoners [3] **Bigorre . . . Rouergue** hamlets in the immediate vicinity of Chinon [4] A. Gellius in Bk. III, *The Attic Nights*, a late Latin collection of notes on grammar, history, philosophy, points of law, and various other topics

Gellius, *li. III, ca. xvi,*

Servius, *in Egl.,* explaining this line from Vergil: *Matri longa decem,* etc.,[5]

and a thousand other fools. Their number has been increased by the lawyers, *ff. De suis et legit., l. Intestato, & fi., &, in Autent., De restitut. & ea que parit in XI mense.*[6] Moreover, they have scribbled over it their bacon-filching law *Gallus, ff. De lib. & posthu., & l. septimo ff. De stat. homi,* and some others which I do not dare to mention at this time. Thanks to these laws, widows can play openly at squeeze-tail whenever they get a bid, and with all their stakes, two months after the death of their husbands.

I beg you graciously, my fine friends, if you should find any worth unbuttoning your breeches for, mount them and bring them to me.

For if they become pregnant in the third month, their offspring will be the heir of the deceased. And so, once they realize they are pregnant, they push boldly on, throwing all caution to the wind since the belly is full. Julia, the Emperor Octavian's daughter, never gave herself to her drummer boys except when she was pregnant, just as a ship takes on its pilot only after it has been caulked and loaded. If anyone should blame them for having themselves patched while pregnant, seeing that animals never allow masculating males on their bellyful, they will reply that that is all right for animals, but that they are women, fully experienced in the fine and merry little rights of superfetation, as Populia replied once, according to Macrobius, *li. II Saturnalia.*

If the devil does not want them pregnant, he will have to twist the spigot and plug the bunghole.

---

[5] **Hippocrates . . . *decem*** Rabelais has borrowed most of his references from the *Attic Nights* of Gellius (III, 16)   [6] *ff . . . mense* Rabelais uses standard symbols in referring to passages from legal texts *ff.* means Justinian's *Digest; l.* means law.

How Gargamelle, Being Pregnant with Gargantua,
Ate a Great Quantity of Tripe

The occasion and the way in which Gargamelle gave birth were the following—and if you don't believe it, may your bottom fall!

Her bottom fell one afternoon, the third day of February, from eating too many *gaudebillaux*. *Gaudebillaux* are the fat tripe from *coiraux*. *Coiraux* are from oxen which have been fattened in the stall and in *grumaulx* meadows. *Grumaulx* meadows are those which bear grass twice a year.[1] Three hundred sixty-seven thousand and fourteen of these fat oxen had been slaughtered and were to be salted down on Shrove Tuesday so that, in the spring, there would be beef aplenty for salty commemoration and in preparation for wine.

The tripe was plentiful, you understand, and so tasty that everyone was licking his fingers. But it would have been a devil of a trick to keep it for long since it would have rotted. This seemed indecent, and so they decided to gulp them down without wasting a mouthful. With this in mind, they invited all the citizens of Cinais, Seuilly, La Roche Clermault, Vaugaudry, without leaving out Coudray-Montpensier, Gué de Vède,[2] and other neighbors, all good drinkers, good companions, and fine ninepin placers.

Good old Grandgousier was enjoying himself immensely, and he directed that the tripe be served by the bowlful. He told his wife, however, that she should eat very little since her term was approaching, and since tripe was not the very best meat. "He would eat shit," he said, "who eats the sack that holds it." Notwithstanding these remonstrances, she ate sixteen hogsheads, two barrels, and six

---

[1] *gaudebillaux . . . grumaulx* are dialect words which Rabelais defines as meticulously as any Sorbonne theologian might define his terms [2] **Cinais . . . Vède** hamlets located near La Devinière

jugs full of it. O what fine fecal matter was to puff up in her!

After dinner, they all went pell-mell to the Saulsaie,[3] and there, on the thick grass, they danced so gaily to the tune of joyful flutes and gentle bagpipes that it was heavenly diversion just to see them having such a good time.

The Remarks of the Drinkers

Then they began talking about having a snack right there. Then bottles hopped, hams trotted, cups flew, pitchers jingled.

"Draw my wine!"

"Give me some!"

"Pour!"

"Water in mine!"

"Give me mine without water . . . that's it, my friend."

"Drink it down in one gulp!"

"Bring out the claret, and make my glass weep!"

"Down with thirst!"

"Ha, false fever, will you not go away?"

"Upon my word, old gal, I just don't seem able to start drinking."

"Are you chilly, my sweet?"

"Yes, I am."

"Saint Cunet's belly![1] Let's talk about drinking."

"I only drink at my hours, like the Pope's mule."[2]

"I only drink from my breviary,[3] like a good father superior."

"Which came first, thirst or drinking?"

"Thirst, for who would have drunk without thirst in the age of innocence?"

---

[3] **Saulsaie** willow grove within sight of La Devinière [1] **Cunet** facetious and obscene name [2] **mule** play on words; mule which carried the pope, and his slipper [3] **breviary** bottles shaped like breviaries actually existed at the time

"Drinking, for *privatio presupponit habitum*,[4] says the law. *Fecundi calices quem non fecere disertum?*" [5]

"We poor innocents drink all too much without thirst."

"I, on the other hand, a sinner, do not drink without thirst. If not a present one, a future one at least; anticipating it, you understand, I drink for the thirst to come. I drink eternally. With me, it's an eternity of drinking, and a drinking of eternity."

"Let's sing, let's drink, let's harmonize in a song."

"Where's my tuner?"

"What! I'm only drinking by proxy!"

"Do you wet your whistle to dry it, or dry it to wet it?"

"I don't know a thing about theory, but I manage to get along in practice."

"Hurry!"

"I moisten, I dampen, I drink, and all out of fear of dying."

"Keep drinking, and you will never die."

"If I don't drink, I'm dry, and there I am dead. My soul will fly away to some frog pond. The soul never dwells in a dry spot."

"Wine-servers, creators of new forms, make me from non-drinking, drinking!"

"A perennial dousing of these dry and withered old bowels!"

"For naught he drinks who feels it not."

"This one's entering my veins . . . the urinal won't get any of it."

"I'd gladly wash the tripe of the calf I dressed this morning."

"My stomach's well ballasted."

"If the paper with my debts on it drank as much as I, my creditors would be stuck when they came around to collect because there would be no trace of writing left."

"Your hand is spoiling your nose."

---

[4] *privatio . . . habitum* privation presupposes custom   [5] *Fecundi . . . disertum* whom do frequent cups not make eloquent

"Oh, how many more will go in before this one comes out!"

"Drink without filling your glass, why that's the way to scrape your snout!"

"This is called a bottle-catcher."

"What's the difference between a bottle and a flagon?"

"A lot. A bottle is closed with a cork and a flagon with a cock."

"That's a good one!"

"Our fathers drank well, and emptied their pots."

"That's turdily sung. Drink up!"

"He's going to wash tripe. Have you something to send to the river?"

"I don't drink any more than a sponge."

"I drink like a Templar."

"And I *tamquam sponsus*." [6]

"And I *sicut terra sine acqua*." [7]

"A synonym for ham?"

"It's a warrant for drinks; it's a pulley. With a pulley you lower wine into the cellar; with ham, into your stomach."

"That's a good one! Give me a drink, hey, a drink there! It's not fully loaded. *Respice personam; pone pro duos; bus non in usu*." [8]

"If I went up as easily as this goes down, I'd have been high in the air long ago."

"That's the way Jacques Coeur[9] got rich."

"That's the way Bacchus conquered India."

"And Philosophy Malindi." [10]

"A little rain lays a big wind. Long drinking routs thunder."

[6] *tamquam sponsus* like a spouse; also pun with preceding "sponge"   [7] *sicut . . . acqua* like land without water   [8] *Respice . . . usu* respect the person, pour for two; *bus* (French for I have drunk) is obsolete. Complicated play on *duobus* and the past tense of the French verb meaning to drink   [9] Jacques Coeur (c. 1395-1456) French merchant who became fabulously rich only to fall into disgrace and ruin   [10] **Malindi** city on the east coast of Africa, discovered by Vasco da Gama

"But if my balls discharged such urine, would you suck them?"

"I hold it in after drinking."

"Fill 'em up boy! I hereby inscribe my name so as not to lose my turn."

"Drink, Will!"

"Is there still another jug?"

"I appeal my condemnation to thirst as an abusive punishment. Boy, take up my appeal in proper form."

"Pass over that last mouthful."

"I used to drink all—now I leave nothing."

"Let's not hurry, and let's be sure not to leave anything."

"Here is some tripe you can bet on, and some chitterlings worthy of a raise in your bid. They come from black-streaked, dun-colored oxen of the region. For God's sake, let's dispatch every bit of it."

"Drink, or I'll . . ."

"No, no!"

"Drink, please."

"Sparrows eat only when you tap their tails. I drink only when I'm properly rubbed."

"*Lagona edatara!* [11] There's not a rabbit-hole in my whole body where this wine is not ferreting out thirst."

"It's whipping mine up very nicely."

"It's going to drive mine away completely."

"Let us proclaim, to the sound of flagons and bottles, that whosoever has lost his thirst should not look for it here—long enemas of drinking have caused it to be emptied out."

"God made planets, and we make plates neat."

"I have God's word in my mouth: *Sitio.*" [12]

"The stone called $\check{\alpha}\beta\epsilon\sigma\tau\sigma\varsigma$[13] is no more inextinguishable than the thirst of my Paternity."

"Appetite comes with eating, Angest du Mans[14] says; thirst goes away with drinking."

---

[11] *Lagona edatara* Basque for Bring me a drink friend [12] *Sitio* I thirst; probable allusion as well to one of Christ's last words [13] $\check{\alpha}\beta\epsilon\sigma\tau\sigma\varsigma$ asbestos [14] **Angest du Mans** Bishop, in his *De causis* (1515)

"A remedy for thirst?"

"It's the opposite of the one for dog-bite—always run after the dog and he will never bite you; always drink before you're thirsty, and it will never catch up to you."

"I caught you! You're asleep. Wake up! Eternal steward, keep us from slumber. Argus[15] had a hundred eyes to see. A steward needs a hundred hands, as Briareus[16] had, in order to pour indefatigably."

"Let's wet our whistle. There's no sense drying out."

"White wine for me. Pour, damn it, pour! Pour over here, fill'er up My tongue's peeling from thirst!"

"Drink up, landsmen!"

"To you, pal, here's to you!"

"Ha! That's gulped down!"

"O lacrima Christi!" [17]

"It's from La Devinière[18]—it's Burgundy grape!"

"What good white wine!"

"And, I swear, it's as smooth as velvet!"

"Ha, ha! but it's good stuff, all wool and a yard wide."

"Take heart, old friend!"

"We're not going to lose this deal because I've taken a trick."

"Ex hoc in hoc." [19] There's no magic, you all saw it. I'm a mass pastor at this kind of thing. Ahem, ahem, I mean I'm a past master."

"Ah, drinkers! Ah, dehydrated ones!"

"Boy, my friend, come here and put a crown of wine on my glass!"

"A cardinal-red one!"

"Natura abhorret vacuum." [20]

"Would you say that a fly would find anything left to drink in my glass?"

---

[15] **Argus** mythological figure with a hundred eyes   [16] **Briareus** mythological figure with a hundred hands   [17] *lacrima Christi* name of an Italian wine   [18] **La Devinière** Rabelais's probable birthplace. It is surrounded by vineyards   [19] *Ex hoc in hoc* from this (the bottle) into that (the glass)   [20] *Natura . . . vacuum* Nature abhors a vacuum

"Bottoms up, as they do in Brittany!"
"Drink it down, every last drop!"
"Swallow, it's good for you! It's a real elixir."

GARGANTUA'S ADOLESCENCE

Gargantua, from the age of three until he was five, was educated and instructed in every proper discipline at his father's orders, and he spent his time just as every child does, that is, in drinking, eating, and sleeping; in eating, sleeping, and drinking; in sleeping, drinking, and eating.

He was always wallowing in the mud, smudging his nose, dirtying his face, running his shoes over at the heels, catching flies with his mouth, and he liked to chase the butterflies over which his father had dominion.[1] He piddled on his shoes, shit in his shirt, blew his nose on his sleeves, dropped snot in his soup, and waddled around everywhere, drank from his slipper, and usually rubbed his belly with a basket. His teeth he sharpened with a wooden shoe, his hands he washed with soup, he combed himself with a cup, sat between two chairs with his rump on the ground, covered himself with a wet sack, drank while eating his soup, ate his cake without bread, bit while laughing, laughed while biting, often spat on his plate, farted from fatness, piddled at the sun, hid in the water to get out of the rain, struck while the iron was cold, daydreamed, was as sweet as sugar, flayed the fox,[2] said the monkey's paternoster,[3] returned to his sheep, turned the sows out to hay, thrashed the servant to teach the master a lesson, put the cart before the horse, scratched himself where it did not itch, wormed secrets out of everyone, embraced too much and grasped little, ate his white bread first, put horseshoes on locusts, tickled himself to make himself laugh, was always rushing to the kitchen, offered

---

[1] **dominion** his father was King of the Butterflies [2] **flayed the fox** vomited [3] **monkey's paternoster** mouthed his prayers

sheaves of straw to the gods, had the *Magnificat* sung at
Matins[4] and found it quite appropriate, ate cabbage and
shitted leeks, was able to recognize a fly in his milk, filled
his days doing nothing, raked paper, smeared parchment,
took to his heels, drank bottoms up, counted without his
host, beat around the bush without getting the bird,
thought that clouds were brass nickels and that kidneys
were lanterns, doubled his money on nothing, played the
ass in order to bray, made a hammer with his fists, captured cranes on the first try, wanted chain mail made link
by link, always looked a gift horse in the mouth, jumped
from cock to bull, robbed Peter to pay Paul, made a ditch
out of dirt, kept the wolf from the door, hoped to catch
larks if the skies fell, made a virtue of necessity, made
soup of bread, cared as little for the shorn as the shaven,
flayed the fox every morning. His father's pups ate out of
his dish; he in turn ate with them. He bit their ears, they
scratched his nose; he blew up their bungholes, they
licked his chops.

And do you know what, my lads? May you be in your
cups if this little lecher wasn't always feeling his nurses,
upside-down, backside frontwards, giddy-up, whoah! And
he was already beginning to exercise his codpiece, which
his nurses decorated every day with pretty bouquets, pretty
ribbons, pretty flowers, pretty tassels. And they spent their
time making it come up between their hands like a sup-
pository. Then they burst out laughing when it lifted its
ears, as if this game had pleased them.

One of them called it my little spout, another my peg,
another my coral branch, another my stopper, my cork, my
plug, my bit, my ramrod, my trunnion, my trinket, my
rough and stiff sport, my lever, my little pink sausage,
my little pooby, booby prize.

"It's mine," said one.

"It's mine," said another.

[4] *Magnificat . . . Matins* this praise of the Virgin is sung only
at Vespers

"How about me?" said another. "Don't I get any? Upon my word, then I'll cut it off."

"Ha, cut it off!" said another, "you would disfigure him, Madame! Are you the kind that cuts off children's tools? He'd be Master Bobtail then."

And so he could play like other little children, they made him a fine whirligig from the wings of a Mirebelais[5] windmill.

How Gargantua was Instructed by a Sophist in Latin Letters

Having realized from his inventiveness how clever a boy he was, Grandgousier was lost in admiration at the good sense and marvelous understanding of his son. And he said to the nurses:

"Phillip, King of Macedonia, became aware of the good sense of his son Alexander from the clever way he handled a horse. Now this horse was so terrible and wild that no one dared to mount it. It had thrown all who had tried: one had his neck broken, another his legs, another his head, another his jawbone. Taking stock of all this in the Hippodrome (which was where they walked and paced their horses), Alexander realized that the horse's fury was simply the result of the fact that it was afraid of its own shadow. And so, mounting it, he made it run against the sun so that the shadow fell behind. In this way, he made the horse respond to his will. His father learned from this of the divine understanding which was in him, and he saw to it that he was thoroughly educated by Aristotle, then the most esteemed of all the Greek philosophers.[1]

"But I can tell from this one conversation which I have just had with my son Gargantua that there is something divine about his understanding.[2] I find him to be so subtle,

[5] **Mirebelais** hamlet in Poitou   [1] Rabelais found this anecdote in Plutarch's *Life of Alexander*   [2] Allusion is to a preceding chapter in which Gargantua demonstrates his marvellous intelligence by inventing a fabulous arse-wipe

profound, and serene that he will certainly reach a supreme degree of wisdom if he is well educated. I want to entrust him for this purpose to some learned man, and I want him to be instructed according to his capabilities. Let no effort be spared."

They had him instructed, therefore, by a great sophist doctor named Master Thubal Holofernes.[3] And he taught him his alphabet so well that he could say it by heart backwards. And he spent five years and three months at this. Then he read to him *Donatus, Facetus, Theodolus,* and Alanus' *In Parabolis.*[4] And he was thirteen years, six months, and two weeks at this.

But note that he taught him to write in Gothic letters[5] in the meantime. And Gargantua wrote out all his books since the art of printing was not yet in use. He usually carried around a big writing desk weighing more than seven hundred thousand pounds. The pen rack alone was as big and thick as the great pillars of Ainay,[6] and the inkhorn hung down from it on huge iron chains strong enough to hold a ton of merchandise.

He then read to him the *De modis significandi*[7] along with the commentaries of Windblow, Porter, Toowordy, Galehad, John Dunce, Badpenny, Pussybumper, and a lot of others. And he was at this for eighteen years and eleven months. He knew them so well that he could repeat them by heart when tested, and he proved to his mother, on his fingers, that *de modis significandi non erat scientia.*[8]

He then read him the *Compost,*[9] and he was sixteen years and two months at this when his preceptor died. And he died in the year fourteen-twenty, of the syphilis which he had aplenty.

After this, he had another old codger, named Master

[8] The name is as Gothic as the system it symbolizes. Sophist is euphemistic for Sorbonne [4] Common medieval textbooks [5] Gothic rather than Roman script [6] Church of St. Martin of Ainay in Lyons had a cupola supported by four huge columns [7] *De modis significandi* on speculative grammar [8] *de . . . scientia* grammar was no science [9] *Compost* a popular almanac

Trussed Juggins.[10] And he read him Hugutio, the *Graecismus* of Everard, the *Doctrinal*, the *Parts*, the *Quid est*, the *Supplementum*, the *Mamotrectus*, the *De moribus in mensa servandis*, Seneca's *De quatuor virtutibus cardinalibus*, Passavantus *cum Commento*, the *Dormi secure*[11] for holy days, and other works of similar grist, the reading of which made him as stuffed as any goose ever baked in an oven.

How Gargantua was Placed under Other Pedagogues

Gargantua's father finally realized that although he was really studying very hard, and spending all his time at it, he was not getting anything out of it, and, worse still, he was becoming a fool, a ninny, a dreamer, and a dunce.

He complained of this to Don Philippe des Marais, Viceroy of Cockaigne,[1] and was told that it would be far better for him to learn nothing than to study such books with such teachers. For their knowledge was only stupidity, and their wisdom only nonsense, and they bastardized good and noble minds and corrupted the flower of youth.

"If you want proof of this," he said, "take any one of these young lads of today who has studied only a couple of years. If he doesn't display better judgment, better speech, better arguments than your son, better bearing and manners, then I'm the biggest bunch of baloney from here to Brenne." [2]

Grandgousier liked this idea very much, and he decided to try it out.

At supper that evening, Des Marais introduced his young page from Villegongis[3] whose name was Eudemon.[4] And

---

[10] Another facetious name [11] *Graecismus . . . secure* school manuals, commentaries on various moral and scriptural questions, and, finally, a book designed to save the preacher the pains of composing his own sermons [1] **Cockaigne** imaginary country of idleness and luxury [2] **Brenne** town in Touraine famous for its meats [3] **Villegongis** town near Châteauroux [4] **Eudemon** name meaning Fortunate in Greek

he was so neatly combed, so well dressed, so well brushed, so open in his manner, that he looked more like a little angel than a man. Then Des Marais said to Grandgousier:

"Do you see this young fellow? He is not yet twelve years old. Let's see, if you will, the difference between the learning of your day-dreaming foologians of yesteryear, and the young men of today."

Grandgousier agreed and bade the page to begin. Eudemon, asking permission of the Viceroy, his master, to do so, with hat in hand, an open face, red lips, self-assured eyes, looking at Gargantua with youthful modesty, stood up and began to praise and commend him—first for his virtues and good manners, secondly for his learning, thirdly his nobility, fourthly his physical beauty, and fifthly, he exhorted him most gracefully to honor and obey his father who was trying so hard to give him a good education. Finally, he begged Gargantua to accept him as the least of his servants, stating that he asked no other gift of heaven at the present moment than that it be given him to serve him in some agreeable way. All this was said with gestures so appropriate, pronunciation so distinct, voice so eloquent and language so elegant, and in such good Latin, that the speaker seemed more like a Gracchus, a Cicero, or an Aemilius[5] of old than a youth of our own day.

Gargantua reacted to all this by bawling like a cow, and hiding his face in his cap. And it was no more possible to get a word out of him than a fart from a dead donkey.

His father was so angry at this that he wanted to kill Master Juggins. But Des Marais restrained him by talking to him in a soothing manner. Grandgousier then instructed that Juggins be paid his wages, given his fill of drink like a good sophist, and then be sent to all the devils in hell.

"For once, at least," he said, "he won't cost his host much if he should die in this state, drunk as a lord."

After Master Juggins had left the house, Grandgousier and the Viceroy talked about possible tutors for Gargantua,

[5] Cicero, the great Roman orator, praises in his *Brutus* both Tiberius Gracchus and Aemilius for their skill in oratory

and they both decided that Ponocrates,[6] Eudemon's
teacher, should have the job, and that all three of them
should go to Paris to see what the youth of France was
learning at that time.

How Gargantua Paid his Welcome to the Parisians and How he Took the Great Bells from the Church of Notre-Dame

A few days later, when they had rested from their trip,
Gargantua went for a tour of the city. He was looked at
in great amazement by everybody; for the people of Paris
are so stupid, so inane, and so foolish by nature that a
juggler, a relic-seller, a mule with bells, a fiddler in the
middle of a public square, will attract a bigger crowd
than a good preacher of the Gospel ever could.

In following him, they harassed him so much that he
was forced to take a rest on the towers of the church of
Notre-Dame. Looking down from there and seeing so many
people standing around, he said in a loud voice:

"I think these rascals expect me to pay my welcome
and my *proficiat*.[1] That's fine. I'm going to give them
wine—but only *par ris*, for fun, that is."

When he finished speaking, smiling, he unfastened his
fine codpiece, and drawing out his pleasure rod, he be-
pissed them so fiercely that he drowned two hundred sixty
thousand, four hundred and eighteen of them, not counting
women and children.

Some escaped this mighty pissflood by fleetness of foot.
And when they reached the highest point of the University,[2] sweating, coughing, spitting, and breathless, they
began to curse and swear, some in anger, others for fun:
"Carymary, carymara! By St. Mamie, we are drenched
par ris." And from that day on the city was called Paris.
It had been called Leucetia before then, as Strabo tells

---

[6] **Ponocrates** means Vigorous   [1] *proficiat* gift offered to a bishop
in welcome   [2] **University** located on the Mount Saint-Geneviève,
a high hill overlooking the Seine

us *lib. iii,* which is to say in Greek, white, because of the white thighs of its ladies. At the imposition of this new name, all present began swearing each one in the name of the saints of his own parish. For Parisians, who are of all kinds and from all places, are by nature both good swearers at, by, or to anything, as well as somewhat presumptuous. It is for this reason that Joaninus de Barranco, *Libro de copiositate reverentiarum,*[3] is of the opinion that they are called *Parrhesians* in Greek, that is, bold-talkers.

Once he had done this, Gargantua inspected the great bells in the tower and started them ringing melodiously. The thought came to him while he was doing this that these bells would look fine on his mare's neck when he sent her back to his father loaded with cheese from Brie and fresh herring. So he carried them home with him.

Meanwhile, a Commander of the Order of St. Anthony came by on his swinish collection.[4] He was tempted to steal these very same bells in order to make himself heard from afar and to make the bacon tremble in the larders. He very honestly left them behind, however, not because they were too precious, but because they were too heavy to carry. This was not the Commander from Bourg, for he is too great a friend of mine to behave in such a way.

The whole city was moved to sedition which, as you know, occurs so frequently that foreign nations are astonished at the patience of the kings of France for not putting a rightful stop to such commotions in view of the disorders they bring about day after day. Would to God I could locate the workshop in which these plots and conspiracies are forged so I could denounce it to the confraternities of my parish!

The place where the crowd congregated, all excited and stirred up, was, as you might guess, Nesle.[5] There was there then, but no longer now, the Oracle of Lutetia.[6]

---

[3] *Libro . . . reverentiarum On the Abundance of Venerable Things,* imaginary author and title   [4] Friars of this order were entitled to donations of ham and bacon   [5] **Nesle** then the seat of the University Court   [6] **Oracle of Lutetia** The Sorbonne

The case was discussed there, and it was demonstrated that it was a misfortune to have the bells carried off. After arguing *pro et contra*, it was concluded in *Baralipton*[7] that the oldest and most capable member of the Faculty should be sent to demonstrate to Gargantua the terrible misfortune caused by the loss of said bells. And, notwithstanding the objections of certain members of the University who maintained that this was a mission that called for an orator rather than a sophist, they selected one Master Janotus de Bragmardo for the job.

How Janotus de Bragmardo was Sent to Recover the Big Bells from Gargantua

Master Janotus, his hair cut like Caesar's,[1] dressed in his antique doctoral gown, his stomach antidoted with cakes from the oven and holy water from the cellar, betook himself to Gargantua's lodgings. Three red-muzzled beadles crawled along ahead of him, and behind him dragged five or six artless masters of arts, all of them as dirty as they could be.

Ponocrates met them at the entrance, and he was frightened when he saw them disguised in this way. He thought that they were witless masqueraders, and he asked one of the artless masters what the meaning of this mummery was. He was informed that they were there to request the return of the stolen bells.

When he heard this, Ponocrates hastened to tell Gargantua the news so that he might prepare an answer and a plan. Gargantua, forewarned, called together his tutor Ponocrates, his steward Philotomus,[2] his squire Gymnastes,[3] and Eudemon, and they began at once to discuss what he should do and reply. They all agreed that the learned doctors should be ushered into the wine cellar

[7] **Baralipton** mnemonic word designating the modes of the first figure of the syllogism   [1] Caesar was bald   [2] **Philotomus** means Lover of Carving in Greek   [3] **Gymnastes** means Teacher of Aesthetics in Greek

and given a good stiff drink. And so the old codger could not boast that the bells had been returned at his request, it was decided that while they were drinking, they would send for the Provost of the City, the Rector of the Faculty, the Vicar to the Bishop, and hand over the bells to them before the sophist had a chance to begin his mission. Once this was done, they would all listen to Janotus' fine speech.

This is precisely what was done, and when the people mentioned above had arrived, the sophist was brought into the room. Wheezing and coughing, he began his speech as follows.

MASTER JANOTUS DE BRAGMARDO'S HARANGUE TO GARGANTUA FOR THE RECOVERY OF THE BELLS

"Ahem, ahem, ahem! *Mna dies,* Sir, *mna dies, et vobis,*[1] Gentlemen. It would be only proper for you to give back our bells, for we have great need of them. Hen, hen, hasch! Already in the past, we have refused good money for them from the inhabitants of London in Cahors, as well as from those of Bordeaux in Brie. They wanted to buy them for the substantific quality of the elementary complexion which is intronificated in the terrestreity of their quiddative nature for extranizing the haloes and the turbines[2] on our vines—not ours, really, but on those round about. For if we lose our wine, we lose everything, both right and reason.

"If you return them at my request, I'll earn six spans of sausage, and a fine pair of breeches which will do my legs a great deal of good. And if I don't, then they'll have broken their promise! Ho! by God, *Domine,*[3] a pair of breeches is good, *et vir sapiens non abhorrebit eam.*[4] Ha, ha! you don't get a pair of breeches just by wishing for

[1] *Mna dies, et vobis* Good-day, and the same to you   [2] Rabelais is making fun here of the Latinized speech of the good doctor   [3] *Domine* Lord   [4] *et . . . eam* and a wise man does not disdain them

them. I know that for a fact. Just think, *Domine,* I've been metagrabolizing[5] this fine speech for eighteen days now. *Redditte que sunt Cesaris Cesari, et que sunt Dei Deo. Ibi jacet lepus.*[6]

"Upon my word, *Domine,* if you want to sup with me *in camera,* by God, *Charitatis, nos faciemus bonum cherubin. Ego occidi unum porcum, et ego habet bon vino.*[7] But of good wine, you can't make bad Latin.

"Moreover, *de parte Dei, date nobis clochas nostras.*[8] Wait, on behalf of the Faculty I'll give you a *Sermones de Utino,*[9] provided that, *utinam,*[10] you give us back our bells. *Vultis etiam pardonos? Per diem, vos habebitis et nihil payabitis.*[11]

"O sir, *Domine, bella givaminor nobis!*[12] Truly, *est bonum urbis.*[13] Everybody needs them. Even if your mare likes them, so does our Faculty, *que comparata est jumentis insipientibus et similis facta est eis, psalmo nescio quo . . .*[14] though I had it jotted down right here in my notebook, *et est unum bonum Achilles.*[15] Hen, hen, ehen, hash!

"Look! I'm going to prove to you that you should give them back to me. *Ego sic argumentor:*[16]

"*Omnis bella bellabilis, in bellerio bellando, bellans*

[5] metagrabolizing pondering [6] *Redditte . . . lepus* Render therefore unto Caesar the things which are Caesar's, and unto God the things which are God's. There's ·the rub [7] *in camera . . . vino* in the guest hall, we shall make good cheer. I have slaughtered a pig, and I have good wine [8] *de parte . . . nostras* by God, give us back our bells [9] *Sermones de Utino* well-known collection (15th cen.) of sermons [10] *utinam* if only [11] *Vultis . . . payabitis* Do you wish pardons as well? By God, you shall have them and pay nothing for them [12] *Domine . . . nobis* Sir, give us back our bells. Bragmardo's speech is primarily in Kitchen Latin, *i.e.* a kind of burlesque composition in which French words are intermixed with Latin words, and with hybrids formed by adding Latin terminations to French words [13] *est . . . urbis* it's the property of the city [14] *que . . . quo* which is comparable to insensible beasts of burden and has been compared to them in I don't know what psalm [15] *et . . . Achilles* it is an invincible argument known in Scholastics as Achilles [16] *Ego . . . argumentor* thus I argue

bellativo bellare bellantes. Parisius habet bellas. Ergo gluc.[17]

"Ha, ha, ha, that's really phrased. It's in *tertio prime, in Darii,*[18] or somewhere else. Upon my soul, I've seen the time when I was a devil of an arguer; but now all I do is dream and think about good wine, a good bed, my back to the fire, my belly to the table, and a good deep dish.

"Hey, *Domine,* I beg you, *in nomine Patris et Filii et Spiritus Sancti, amen,*[19] to give us back our bells. And may God keep you from harm, and our Lady of Health, *qui vivat et regnat per omnia secula seculorum, amen.*[20] Hem, hasch, ahash, grraasshh!

"*Verum enim vero, quando quidem, dubio procul, edepol, quoniam, ita certe, meus Deus fidus,*[21] a city without bells is like a blind man without a cane, a donkey without a crupper, a cow without a bell. Until you have given them back, we'll not stop crying after you like a blind man who has lost his cane, to bray like a donkey without a crupper, and to bellow like a cow without a bell.

"A certain Latinist, living near the Municipal Hospital, once said, on the authority of one Taponus—I beg your pardon, I mean Pontanus, the secular poet[22]—that he wished bells were made of feathers and their clappers of fox tails because they gave him the chronic—er, I mean, colic—in the tripes of his brain when he composed his carminiformal [23] lines. But, bing, bang, bong, bom, bom,

---

[17] *Omnis . . . gluc* Every bellable bell, to be belled in the belfrey, belling by the bellative, makes the bellers bell bellfully. Paris has bells. There's the proof (*ergo gluc* is a formula used in concluding a demonstration) I have given the English equivalent of Rabelais's Kitchen Latin [18] *tertio . . . Darii* this argument is in the third mode of the first figure of the syllogism, in the category called Darii [19] *in nomine . . . amen* in the name of the Father and of the Son and of the Holy Spirit, amen [20] *qui vivat . . . amen* who lives and reigns for ever and ever [21] *Verum . . . fidus* but in truth whereas indubitably, by Pollux, since thus certainly, my God who is my faith. Series of stock Latin phrases [22] **Pontanus** Italian humanist poet (15th cen.) [23] **carminiformal** in verse form

bom, he was declared a heretic . . . we turn them out as easy as pie. And the deponent has had his say. *Valete et plaudite. Calepinus recensui.*" [24]

How the Sophist Carried off his Cloth, and How he Brought Suit Against the other Masters

The sophist had no sooner finished than Ponocrates and Eudemon burst out laughing so hard that they thought that they were going to give up the ghost, just as Crassus did when he saw a big-balled ass eating thistles, or Philemon who died from laughter when he saw an ass eating the figs that had been prepared for his dinner. Master Janotus began to laugh too, and they all laughed so much that their eyes watered from the violent concussion of the substance of the brain which caused the lachrymal humidities to be squeezed out and run down the optic nerves. Here was a fine example of Democritus heraclitizing, and of Heraclitus democratizing.[1]

When they finally stopped laughing, Gargantua consulted with his followers as to what they ought to do. Poncrates was of the opinion that they should give another drink to this excellent orator. Moreover, seeing that he had provided them with amusement, and had made them laugh more than Songecreux, the famous comedian, he thought that they should provide him with the ten spans of sausage Janotus mentioned in his gleeful harangue, as well as a pair of breeches, three hundred big logs of cordwood, twenty-five barrels of wine, a bed with a three-layer goose feather mattress, and a very deep and capacious bowl—all those things he had declared necessary for his old age.

Everything was done just as it had been decided, except that Gargantua, doubting that they would be able to find right then and there breeches suitable for his legs, uncertain as well which cut would be the best for said

[24] *Valete . . . recensui* Goodbye and applaud. I Calepinus (Italian monk, author of a dictionary) have spoken   [1] **Democritus**, Greek philosopher, named the Laughing Philosopher; **Heraclitus**, known as the Weeping Philosopher

orator—the martingale, which has a drawbridge effect in the seat so that one can do one's duty more easily, or the sailor style, which is more comfortable for the kidneys, or the Swiss style, which is warmer for the paunch, or the codfish-tail type, which is cooler on the loins—not knowing which of these to give him, he presented him with seven ells of black cloth and three of white for the lining. The porters carried the wood, the masters of arts carried the sausages and bowls, while Master Janotus insisted upon carrying the cloth himself.

One of the masters, Jousse Bandouille, protested that this was neither respectable nor decent for one of his rank, and that he should hand the cloth over to one of them.

"Ha!" said Janotus, "Blockhead, blockhead, you have not concluded *in modo et figura.*[2] What's the sense of having the *Suppotiones* and the *Parva Logicalia? Panus pro quo supponit?*" [3]

"*Confuse,*" said Bandouille, "*et distributive.*" [4]

"I didn't ask you, blockhead," said Janotus, "*quo modo supponit,* but *pro quo;*[5] the answer, blockhead, is *pro tibiis meis.*[6] And for this reason, I'll carry it *egomet, sicut suppositum portat adpositum.*" [7]

And so off he carried it, as stealthily as Patelin[8] in the farce.

The best part of all was when the old wheezer, in full session of the Faculty held in the Church of the Mathurins,[9] requested his breeches and sausages. His colleagues turned down his request peremptorily with the statement that, according to their information, he had already got them from Gargantua. Janotus protested that

[2] *in . . . figura* according to the principles of formal logic
[3] *Suppotiones . . . supponit Relations* and the *Little Treatise on Logic.* To what is the cloth related? The *Suppotiones* form a section of the *Parva logicalia* [4] *et . . . distributive* its relation is general and particular to no one [5] *quo . . . quo* how it is related, but to what [6] *pro . . . meis* to my legs [7] *egomet . . . adpositum* myself, just as the substance carries the attribute [8] **Patelin** crafty hero of a 15th century French farce of the same name [9] this is where the Sorbonne held its general assemblies

they had been given him *gratis*, and out of pure generosity, and that this in no wise absolved them of their promises. They told him, nevertheless, that he should be happy with what was just, and that he would not get one drop more.

"Justice," said Janotus, "we never have any of that here! Miserable traitors, you are worthless. There are no more wicked creatures on the face of the earth than you, that I know for sure. Never limp in the presence of the lame. I'm just one of you when it comes to wickedness. By God's spleen, I'll inform the King of the enormous abuses perpetrated here in your hands and heads, and I'll be a scurvy rascal if he doesn't have you all burned alive as buggers, traitors, heretics, seducers, enemies of God and of virtue!"

Upon hearing these words, the Faculty drew up an indictment against him; he, in turn, had them served summonses. In short, the case went to court, and it's there yet. The members of the Faculty, at this juncture, made a vow not to wash themselves; Master Janotus and his adherents made a vow not to blow their noses until a final decision on the matter was handed down.

Because of these vows they have remained dirty and snotty right up to the present day, for the Court has not yet examined all the documents in detail. The decision will be handed down at the next Greek Calends, that is to say, never. For, as you know, they go farther than nature and contrary to their own laws. The laws of Paris keep chirping that only God can perform infinite things. Nature can make nothing immortal, and she assigns a term and an end to everything she produces: for *omnia orta cadunt*, etc.[10] But these fog-swallowing loafers make cases pending both infinite and immortal. In so doing, they justify and verify the words of Chilo the Lacedaemonian, consecrated at Delphos, to the effect that Misery is the companion of Lawsuit, and that people who plead are miserable for they attain the end of their lives sooner than the satisfaction of their rights.

[10] *omnia . . . cadunt* all things born have an end

The Education of Gargantua under the Direction of his Sophist Teachers

This took up the first few days. Once the bells were put back in place, the citizens of Paris, out of gratitude for Gargantua's honorable action, offered to keep and feed his mare for as long as he wished. Gargantua accepted this courtesy, and the Parisians sent the animal to graze in the Forest of Fontainebleau. I don't believe she's still there.

Now Gargantua expressed a heartfelt desire to begin studying at Ponocrates' discretion, but he directed him to continue in his usual manner in order to learn in what way, for such a long time, his former teachers had made him so dumb, stupid, and ignorant.

Gargantua disposed of his time, therefore, as he ordinarily did, getting out of bed between eight and nine in the morning whether it was light out or not. This is what his former tutors instructed him to do, and they referred to the words of David: *Vanum est vobis ante lucem surgere.*[1]

Then he wiggled, flopped, wallowed in his bed a bit in order to revive his animal spirits. He got dressed, according to the season, except that he always wanted to wear a big long gown of thick wool, lined with fox fur. Then he combed his hair with Almain's comb—with four fingers and a thumb, that is—for his tutors maintained that to comb one's hair, to wash one's face, to wear clean clothes, were a waste of time in this world.

Then he did his business, piddled, vomited, belched, broke wind, yawned, spat, coughed, hiccoughed, sneezed, and blew his nose like an arch-deacon. He then had breakfast so as to fortify himself against the morning dew and the foul air. His menu consisted of fine fried tripe, choice grilled meats, hams, fine roast kid, and a plentiful supply of good, rich convent soup.

[1] *Vanum . . . surgere* It is useless for you to rise before the light. Quotation is from Psalm LXXVI; its original meaning is distorted in this context

Ponocrates pointed out that he really ought not to eat so soon after getting out of bed without having a little exercise first. Gargantua replied:

"What! have I not exercised sufficiently? I wallowed around in bed six or seven times before getting up. Isn't that enough? Pope Alexander did the same, at the advice of his Jewish physician, and he lived until the day of his death in spite of his enemies. My first teachers got me into the habit. They claimed that breakfast was good for the memory, and so they started off the day by drinking. It doesn't bother me one bit, and I eat all the more at dinner. Master Tubal Holofernes (who was at the head of his class in Paris) told me that there is no advantage in running fast, but, rather, in leaving early. The total health of mankind does not reside in drinking, drinking, drinking, like ducks, but, rather, early in the morning; *unde versus:*[2]

> To rise in the morning is gray,
> To drink in the morning is gay.

After a hearty breakfast, Gargantua went off to church, and he was brought, in a large basket, a huge breviary swaddled in velvet, weighing with its grime, clasps, and parchment eleven hundred and six pounds, give or take a pound. He heard twenty-six to thirty masses there. In the meantime his chaplain came in, tucked in his hood like a peewit in his feathers, with his breath well antidoted with much syrup from the vine. With him, Gargantua mumbled all his litanies, and he picked them so carefully that not one morsel fell to the ground.

Upon leaving the church, he was brought an oxcart loaded down with rosaries, each bead bigger than a hatblock, and he walked through the cloisters, galleries, and gardens saying more of them than sixteen hermits.

Then he studied a miserly half-hour, his eyes glued to the book, but (as the comic poet[3] says) his soul was in the kitchen.

After filling a large urinal, he sat down at table and,

[2] **unde versus** whence the lines   [3] Terence, *Eunuch,* IV, 8

since he was naturally phlegmatic, began his meal with a few dozen hams, smoked beef tongues, caviar, sausages, and other such forerunners of wine.

While he did this, four of his servants, one after the other, continuously shovelled mustard into his mouth. Then he drank a horrific draught of white wine to relieve the kidneys. Then he ate, according to the season, meats to his liking. And he stopped only when his belly had reached the bursting point.

When it came to drinking, he had neither end nor rule, for, he said, the limits and bounds of drinking were when, the person drinking, the cork in his shoes swelled up half a foot from the ground.

GARGANTUA'S GAMES

Then, mumbling ponderously a bit of grace, he washed his hands in cool wine, picked his teeth with a pig's foot, and conversed gaily with his men. They then spread a green cloth, brought out playing cards, dice and boards.[1]

After playing, straining, passing and winnowing his time, it was only proper to drink a little—that meant eleven sixteen-gallon bumpers per man—and, immediately after supper, to stretch out on a fine bench or in a fine bed, and sleep for two or three hours without thinking or speaking a thing.

On awakening, he wiggled his ears a little. Meanwhile they brought him fresh wine, and he drank more heartily than ever.

Ponocrates remonstrated that it was not good for him to drink so much immediately upon waking.

"Such is the true life of the Fathers," he replied, "for my sleep is naturally salty; sleep has the same effect on me as ham."

Then he began to study a bit, and out came his beads. He mounted an old mule which had served nine kings in

[1] There follows a list of some 220 different games which I have had to exclude because of limitations of space

order to dispatch them in proper form. With a great deal of mumbling of the mouth and doddling of the head, he went off to see some rabbit caught in a trap.

Upon his return, he went to the kitchen to see what kind of roast was on the spit. And he supped very well, I assure you. Sometimes he invited some of his drinking companions whom he matched drink for drink, story for story, both old and new. The Lords of Fou, Gourville, Grignault, and Marigny[2] were among his servants.

After supper pretty wooden gospels were set up—that is to say, a number of game boards. And they played *One, Two, Three* or, to finish up, *Everything Goes.* Or 'they went to visit the lasses of the neighborhood, with an occasional light banquet, collation, and post-collation thrown in for good measure. Then, without interruption, Gargantua slept until eight o'clock the following morning.

How Gargantua was Instructed by Ponocrates so as not to Waste a Single Hour of the Day

When Ponocrates got to know Gargantua's depraved way of life, he decided to plan a different course of instruction for him; but he let him go his own way for a few days, realizing that Nature cannot endure sudden changes without great violence.

The better to begin his work, he requested a learned physician of the day, one Master Theodore,[1] to consider whether it would be possible to put Gargantua on the right course. He proceeded to purge him canonically with Anticyrian hellebore,[2] and this treatment cleansed his mind of its unnatural and perverse habits. Ponocrates, by this means also, made him forget all he had learned from his former teachers, just as Timotheus[3] did when he took on pupils who had been taught by other musicians.

[2] *Fou . . . Marigny* all real people, contemporaries of Rabelais
[1] **Theodore** name meaning God Given [2] **hellebore** considered a remedy for madness by the Ancients; so called from the Greek island of Anticyra [3] **Timotheus** famous musician of Antiquity

In order to provide the proper motivation, Ponocrates introduced him into the company of learned men. Their example served to increase his inclination and desire to study in a different manner, and to make full use of his talents. Ponocrates then put him on such a schedule that not a moment of the day was lost, and all of his time was spent in the pursuit of learning and knowledge.

Gargantua began getting up, therefore, at about four in the morning. While he was being massaged, he listened to passages from Holy Scripture, read to him aloud in a distinct voice, and pronounced with fitting respect for the text. A young page, Anagnostes,[4] who was a native of Basché,[5] was appointed reader. According to the subject or argument of the lesson, Gargantua frequently turned to reverence, adore, pray, and worship the good Lord, whose majesty and marvelous judgment were made manifest in the reading.

Next, he repaired to a secret place to attend to the natural excretory functions of the body. Here his teacher repeated what had been read, and explained the more obscure and difficult points. Returning, they studied the heavens, noticing whether they were the same as on the preceding night, and what signs the sun and moon were entering into that day.

Afterwards, Gargantua was dressed, combed, curled, trimmed, and perfumed, and, while this was going on, he heard once again the lessons of the day before. Saying them by heart himself, and using them as a point of departure, he made practical application of them to things human. This went on sometimes for two or three hours, but Gargantua usually stopped once he was fully dressed.

Then, for three solid hours, he was read to. After this, they went outside, and continuing their discussion of the subjects in the readings, they went to the tennis court at Bracque, or to the fields. And they played ball, tennis, or

[4] **Anagnostes** name meaning Reader [5] **Basché** hamlet near Chinon

three-cornered catch, exercising their bodies as vigorously as they had exercised their minds before.

Their playing was relaxed and easy since they quit whenever they felt like it, and they usually stopped once they had worked up a good sweat or were exhausted. Then they were thoroughly dried and rubbed down, after which they changed their shirts and walked quietly home to see if dinner were ready. As they waited, they recited clearly and eloquently such quotations as they remembered from the morning reading.

Meanwhile, My Lord Appetite put in an appearance, and they all sat down opportunely.

At the beginning of the meal, there was a reading from some pleasant story of chivalry in days gone by, and this lasted until Gargantua gave the signal for the wine to be served.

Then, if he wished, the reading was continued, or they began to chat with one another merrily. At first they discussed the virtues, properties, nature, and efficacy of everything that was served them: bread, wine, water, salt, meat, fish, fruit, roots, herbs, and their preparation. In this way, Gargantua soon learned all the related passages in Pliny, Athenaeus, Dioscordes, Julius Pollux, Galen, Porphyry, Oppian, Polybius, Heliodorus, Aristotle, Aelian,[6] and others. As they talked about these subjects, so as to be sure of their points, they often had the books in question brought to the table. And Gargantua remembered so well and so completely everything that was said that there was not a physician anywhere who knew one half as much as he.

They then discussed the lessons which had been read in the morning, and, topping his meal off with a bit of quince marmalade, Gargantua cleaned his teeth with a piece of mastic, washed his hands and eyes in cool, clear water, and gave thanks to God with noble hymns composed in praise of the divine munificence and goodness.

[6] **Pliny . . . Aelian** all these ancient authors wrote on natural history

They then brought in cards, not for playing, but that they might learn a thousand little points and fine inventions, all based on arithmetic.

In this way, Gargantua became fond of the science of numbers, and every day, after dinner and after supper; he spent his time at this with as much pleasure as he formerly derived from dicing and gaming. The result of this was then he learned so much about mathematical theory and practice that the Englishman Tunstal,[7] who had written extensively on the subject, confessed that actually, in comparison with Gargantua, he knew no more about mathematics than about Old High German.

The same was true of the other mathematical sciences, such as geometry, astronomy, and music. For as they waited for their meal to digest, they constructed a thousand amusing instruments and geometric figures, and practiced as well the principles of astronomy.

Then they had great fun singing in four- or five-part harmony, or in improvising on a theme which they liked. As for musical instruments, Gargantua learned to play the lute, the spinet, the harp, the German flute with nine holes, the viol, and the trombone.

Having spent an hour at this, his digestion being completed, he discharged his natural excrements and then went back to his principal studies for three hours or more. He either repeated the morning reading, or went on with the book he had begun, or practiced writing, drawing and forming letters in the ancient Roman script.

Then they left the house with a young gentleman from Touraine, Squire Gymnastes, who taught Gargantua the equestrian arts. Changing his clothes, he proceeded to mount a courser, a charger, a jennet, a Berber, a light, fleet-footed steed. And he put them through their paces, making them leap in the air, cross a ditch, jump a hurdle, turn about in a circle, both to the left and to the right.

He never broke a lance, for it is the most stupid thing in the world to boast: "I have broken ten lances in a tilt

[7] **Tunstal** (1476-1559) author of a treatise on arithmetic

or fight." A carpenter can do as much. But it is a laudable thing to break ten enemies with one lance. Holding his steel-tipped lance stiff and firm, Gargantua split a door, pierced a coat of mail, felled a tree, snarled a ring, picked up an army saddle, a hauberk or a gauntlet. And he did all these things armed from head to toe.

As for prancing his horse and making all the proper sounds, no one was his equal. The celebrated jockey of Ferrara[8] was a mere monkey in comparison. He learned, too, to leap quickly from one horse to another without touching the ground—these horses were called "desultories"—and he mounted from either side, lance in hand, without stirrups, and guided his horse at will without a bridle; for such accomplishments as these are part of military training.

Another day he practiced with the battle-axe. And he handled it so well, with such powerful swings and encircling sweeps, that he was a master knight-in-arms on the field and in all trials of strength.

Then he brandished the pike, plied the two-handed sword, the bastard sword, the Spanish rapier, the dagger and the poniard, armed or unarmed, equipped with his buckler, with his cloak, with a small round shield.

He hunted stag, roebuck, bear, doe, wild boar, hare, partridge, pheasant, otter. He played with a heavy ball, made it bound in the air with his foot as well as with his fist. He wrestled, ran, jumped—not three steps and a jump, not the hop-step-and-jump, not the German jump, for, as Gymnastes pointed out, those jumps are useless and of no account in war—but, with one leap, he bounded over a ditch, vaulted over a hedge, or ran six paces straight up the side of a wall and climbed in this manner to a window the height of a lance from the ground.

He swam in deep water, on his belly, on his back, on his side, with his whole body, with his feet alone; one hand in the air, holding up a book, he crossed the River

[8] **Jockey of Ferrara** a certain Cesare Fieschi

Seine without getting it wet, dragging his cloak along in his teeth, as Julius Caesar did. Then with one hand, he hoisted himself bodily into a boat; from the boat he dived back into the water head first, sounded out the bottom, grazed the rocks, plunged into the pits and caverns. Then he turned the boat, steered it, propelled it swiftly, slowly, upstream, downstream, held it steady in the strongest current, guided it with one hand, plied a big oar with the other, spread the sail, climbed the mast by the rigging, ran along the yards, adjusted the compass, set the ropes against the wind, held the steering wheel firm.

Coming out of the water, he climbed straight up a mountain, and came back down with the same speed, climbed trees like a cat, jumped from one to the other like a squirrel, and felled huge limbs like another Milo.[9] With two steel pointed poniards and a pair of strong punchers, he scurried to the top of a house like a rat, then came down again from roof to ground in such a fashion that he was not hurt one bit by his fall.

He threw the dart, the bar, the stone, the javelin, the boar-spear, and the halberd; he drew the bow, and stretched to the breaking point a huge ballista,[10] sighted the arquebus, mounted the cannon, shot at targets, clay pigeons, from top to bottom, from bottom to top, from the front, from the side, from behind like the Parthians.[11]

They tied a cable to a high tower for him, and let it dangle to the ground. He climbed this, hand over hand, and then slipped down it more evenly and surely than you could have on a perfectly flat field.

They set up a large pole between two trees for Gargantua to hang from by his hands. And he went back and forth along it, so swiftly, without letting his feet touch anything, that running at top speed on the ground below, you could not have kept up with him.

To exercise his chest and lungs, he shouted like all the

[9] **Milo** famed Greek athlete   [10] **ballista** siege engine shaped like a cross bow, used for hurling missiles   [11] **Parthians** who turned on their horses and shot their arrows at the pursuing enemy

devils in hell. And I heard him call Eudemon once from the Porte Saint-Victor all the way to Montmartre.[12] Stentor[13] himself did not have such a voice at the battle of Troy.

To develop his muscles, they made him a pair of heavy salmon-shaped lead pieces, each weighing eight hundred and seventy thousand pounds, which Gargantua called dumbbells. Taking one in each hand, he lifted them off the ground, raised them in the air over his head, and held them there, without moving, three quarters of an hour or more. This is an inimitable feat of strength.

He played tug-of-war with the strongest, and he was so firm on his feet when it came to the test that he defied even the sturdiest to budge him. In this he emulated Milo[14] of old, who held a pomegranate in his hand and gave it to anyone who could take it from him.

Having spent his time in this manner, and once he was rubbed down, washed, and refreshed with a change of clothing, he returned home at a leisurely pace. Passing through meadows or other grassy spots, Gargantua and his companions inspected the trees and plants, compared them with the descriptions the Ancients made of them, such as Theophrastus, Dioscorides, Marinus, Pliny, Nicander, Macer, and Galen.[15] They took handfuls of them home where a young page called Rhizotome[16] took charge of them, along with the mattocks, picks, hoes, spades, pruning knives, and other instruments required for proper botanizing.

Once they were at home, while dinner was being prepared, they repeated a few of the passages that had been read; then they sat down at table.

It is to be noted here that dinner was sober and frugal,

[12] That is, from one end of Paris to the other [13] **Stentor** Trojan herald in the *Iliad,* famous for his loud voice [14] **Milo** of Crotona, famous Greek athlete [15] All, except Marinus, known for his work on anatomy, were Greek and Latin authors of treatises on botany [16] **Rhizotome** name meaning Root Cutter

for Gargantua ate only enough at that time to muzzle the barkings of his stomach. But his supper was large and copious since he took as much as needed for his sustenance and nourishment. This is the true diet prescribed by good and sure medical art, although a lot of blockhead doctors, wrangling in the claptrap of the sophists, recommend the exact opposite.

The reading begun at dinner was continued during this meal as long as it was thought proper. The remainder of the time was spent in literate and useful conversation.

After grace was said, they began to sing tunefully, to play instruments harmoniously, to amuse themselves with such light pastimes as cards, dice, and dice cups. And they kept this up, having a good time and enjoying themselves, oftentimes until they were ready for bed. Frequently they went and called on learned men, or on people who had travelled in foreign lands.

When night came, before going to bed, they went to the most open place in the house in order to see the face of the sky. They studied the comets, if there were any, and the shape, situation, aspect, opposition, and conjunction of the stars.

Then Gargantua recapitulated briefly with his teacher, in the manner of the Pythagoreans, all he had read, seen, learned, done, and heard in the course of the whole day.

Afterwards, he prayed to God the Creator, adoring Him, confirming his faith in Him, glorifying Him for His immense bounty, thanking Him for all time past, and commending himself to His divine clemency for all time to come.

This done, he retired to bed.

How Gargantua Spent the Time in Rainy Weather

In intemperate and rainy weather, Gargantua spent the time before dinner in the usual way, but a big, bright fire was lighted to correct the inclemency of the air. After dinner, instead of outdoor exercises, he stayed in the house, and for apotherapy,[1] spent the time baling hay, splitting and sawing wood, threshing sheaves in the barn. Then he studied the arts of painting and sculpture, or revived the ancient game of Tali, or dice, as Leonicus[2] has described it, and as our good friend Lascaris[3] plays it. And as they played, they recalled passages from ancient authors where there is some mention of, or some metaphor applicable to this game.

They also went to see how metals were forged or artillery cast; or they went to see the lapidaries, goldsmiths, and carvers of precious stones; or alchemists, money coiners, upholsterers, weavers, velvet-workers, watch makers, looking glass makers, printers, organists, dyers, and other such workmen. They distributed gratuities wherever they went, and they learned about and inspected the invention and industry of the various trades.

They attended and listened to public lectures, official convocations, oratorical performances, speeches, pleadings by eloquent attorneys, and sermons by evangelical preachers.

They frequented fencing halls, and Gargantua put his skill at all the weapons to the test, taking on the masters, proving to them that he knew as much about them as they, and even more.

And, instead of botanizing, they visited the shops of druggists, herbalists, and apothecaries, studiously observing the fruits, roots, leaves, gums, seeds, exotic ointments, as well as the manner in which they were adulterated.

They went to see the jugglers, mountebanks, and medicasters, watching their gestures, their tricks, their antics, and their fine banter, especially those from Chauny in Picardy, for they are born chatterers, and the finest flaunters of foolishness in matters of green monkeys.[4]

Coming back for supper, they ate more soberly than on

[1] apotherapy exercise [2] Leonicus Italian humanist, author of a dialogue on the subject [3] Lascaris Greek scholar and contemporary of Rabelais [4] green monkeys do not exist

other days. And they had food that was more desiccative and extenuating so as to counteract the humidity communicated to their bodies by the necessary contiguity of the atmosphere, and so as to nullify any harm that might arise from lack of their customary exercise.

Such was Gargantua's program, and he kept it up from day to day, profiting from it as much as one would expect any young man of his age and intelligence who applied himself faithfully to such a schedule. Although it seemed difficult for him at the beginning, it soon became, as he went on, so pleasant, easy, and delightful that it was more like the pastime of a king than the curriculum of a student.

Ponocrates, however, in order to relieve the intense mental concentration, chose, once a month, some clear, fine day on which they left the city, early in the morning, for Gentilly, or Boulogne, or Montrouge, or the Pont de Charenton, or Vanves, or Saint-Cloud.[5] And they spent the whole day there, enjoying themselves to the utmost, laughing, joking, drinking their fill, playing, singing, dancing, gamboling in some fair meadow, hunting sparrows' nests, catching quails, fishing for frogs and crayfish.

But even though they spent the day without books and reading, they did not spend it without profit; for, lying in a green meadow, they recited from memory delightful lines from Vergil's *Georgics,* from Hesiod, from Politian's *Rusticus,*[6] and composed amusing epigrams in Latin which they subsequently turned into rondelets or ballads in French.

When they ate lunch, they separated the water from the wine in the manner taught by Cato in his *De re rust.*[7] and by Pliny, that is, by pouring it into a cup of ivy-wood; they washed the wine in a basin full of water and drew it off with a funnel; they passed the water from one glass to another, and they constructed little automatic devices, that is to say, which worked by themselves.

[5] Gentilly . . . Saint-Cloud all within the immediate vicinity of Paris [6] *Georgics . . . Rusticus* in praise of the joys of the country [7] *De re rust.* On Husbandry

How there Arose between the Bakers of Lerne and Gargantua's Countrymen the Great Quarrel from which Sprang Fierce Wars

At that time, which was the vintage season, at the beginning of autumn, the shepherds of the country were guarding the vines and keeping the starlings from eating the grapes.

At this very time, the bakers of Lerné[1] happened to be passing along the highway, on their way to town with ten or a dozen loads of cakes.

Our shepherds asked them courteously to sell them some of their cakes at the current market price. For do not forget that grapes and freshly baked cakes make a most heavenly breakfast—especially Burgundy, fig-grapes, muscat, arbor grapes, and black diarrhetic ones for those who are constipated and which make you squirt the length of a long pole. Those who eat them, thinking to pass wind, frequently pass something else. They are known as vintage-thinkers for this reason.

The bakers were not one bit inclined to grant the shepherds their request, and (which was worse) they insulted them terribly, calling them scum of the earth, toothless idiots, red-headed Judases, lechers, bedpoopers, brats, sneaky dogs, lazy pigs, fags, pot-bellies, braggards, stinkers, clodhoppers, clots, blowhards, sissies, monkey faces, lazy louts, bums, boobs, scoundrels, simpletons, silly jokers, duds, teeth chattering dopes, dirty cowherds, dung-dipping shepherds, and other such defamatory epithets. And they added that dainty cakes were not for the likes of them, that they should be satisfied with coarse bread or lumpy loaves.

To this outrage, one of the shepherds, Frogier by name, a fine, honest young lad, replied calmly:

"Since when did you begin to sprout horns that you've

---

[1] Lerné village near La Devinière

become so arrogant? Tell me, didn't you always use to sell us your cakes? And now you refuse? That's not very neighborly of you. Do we act that way when you come here to buy our fine wheat from which you make your cakes? Besides, we would have thrown some of our grapes into the bargain. But, by God, you'll be sorry for what you've done when the time comes for you to call on us. Then we'll treat you in the same way, and don't you forget it!"

Then Marquet, standard-bearer of the bakers' confraternity, said to him:

"You're certainly pretty cocky this morning; you must have eaten too much millet last evening. Step up, step up, I'll give you some of my cake!"

Then Frogier, in all candor, started towards him, drawing a ten-penny piece from his belt, imagining only that Marquet was going to give him some cakes. But Marquet lashed him across the legs so fiercely with his whip that he raised large welts. Then he tried to run away; but Frogier yelled murder and help as loud as he could. At the same time, he threw at him a big club he was carrying under his arm, and it struck him on the head, at the coronal juncture, on the right side, under the crotaphite or temporal artery,[2] causing him to fall from his mare more dead than alive.

Meanwhile, the farmers, who were nearby knocking down nuts, ran up with their long poles and began to beat the bakers as though they were threshing green rye. The other shepherds and shepherdesses, hearing Frogier's cries, came with their slings and catapults, and chased them with stones that flew as fast and thick as hail. They finally caught up to them, and took from them about four or five dozen cakes. They paid the customary price for them, however, and gave them in addition a hundred nuts and three basketfuls of white grapes. The bakers proceeded to help Marquet mount again—he was badly hurt—and they all returned then to Lerné, without going on to Parilly, heap-

[2] This is Rabelais, the physician, speaking

ing dire threats as they went on the herders, shepherds, and farmers of Seuilly and Cinais.[3]

When they were gone, the shepherds and shepherdesses feasted on their cakes and fine grapes, danced to the sound of pipes, and laughed at those proud bakers who had had the worst of it because they had crossed themselves with the wrong hand that morning. And they bathed Frogier's legs so lovingly in the juice of large white and black grapes that he was cured in no time at all.

How the Inhabitants of Lerné under the Command of Picrochole, their King, Assaulted Gargantua's Shepherds without Warning

The bakers, upon returning to Lerné, did not pause to eat or drink, but went immediately to the Capitol. There, in the presence of their king, Picrochole,[1] third of that name, they set forth their grievances, showed their broken baskets, their tattered bonnets, their ripped cloaks, their plundered cakes, and especially Marquet, horribly wounded, and said that all this had been done by Grandgousier's shepherds and farmers, near the great highway, beyond Seuilly.

Picrochole, immediately, without stopping to consider the circumstances or to inform himself further, flew into a furious rage. He sounded the ban and arrière-ban[2] throughout the country, summoned everyone, on pain of hanging, to assemble under arms in the great square in front of the castle at noon.

In order to make doubly sure of his enterprise, he had the alarm drum beaten all over the town. He himself, while his dinner was being prepared, saw to it that his

---

[3] The Picrocholine War takes place in the countryside around Rabelais's birthplace, and all the localities mentioned have been located on the map of that region   [1] **Picrochole** name meaning Black Bile   [2] **ban and arrière-ban** royal edict summoning vassals to military service

artillery was mounted, his standard and banner run up, and a quantity of munitions, armor, and rations put in readiness.

During dinner, he distributed his commissions, and, by his command, Lord Shagrag was put in charge of the vanguard, which consisted of sixteen thousand fourteen harquebusiers, and thirty-five thousand eleven volunteer infantrymen.

My Lord Squire Braggart was placed in charge of the artillery, which included nine hundred and fourteen pieces of bronze in cannons, double cannons, basilisks, serpentines, culverins, siege guns, falcons or small cannon, light artillery, small culverins, and others. The rearguard was commanded by the Duke of Scratchpenny, while the King and the Princes of the blood were in the main army.

Thus hastily organized, before setting out, they dispatched three hundred light horses under the command of Captain Suckwind to reconnoiter and to look for possible ambush. But their diligent search revealed only a country in peace and silence, without a sign of gathering of any kind.

Upon hearing this, Picrochole commanded each unit to march forward at once under its colors. So they took to the field without order or discipline, despoiling and laying waste everything they encountered, sparing neither poor nor rich, sacred place nor profane. They carted off oxen, cows, bulls; calves, heifers, lambs; sheep, goats, ewes; hens, capons, pullets; goslings, ganders, geese; hogs, sows, and pigs. They knocked down nuts, spoiled vines, carried off stocks and stripped the trees of their fruit. They wrought an indescribable havoc, and there was no one to resist them. Each and every one threw himself on their mercy, begging to be treated humanely in view of the fact that they had always been good and friendly neighbors, and had never committed any kind of excess or outrage against them which could possibly justify such mistreatment, and they added that God would speedily punish them.

The only answer that Picrochole's men made to these remarks was that they would teach them how to eat cakes.

How a Monk of Seuilly Saved the Abbey Close from Being Ravaged by the Enemy

Thieving, pillaging, plundering along the way, they finally reached Seuilly,[1] where they robbed both men and women of all their possessions. Nothing was too hot or heavy for them. Although the plague was in most of the houses, they went in everywhere and carried off everything there was. And not a single one of them caught the pestilence. This is quite miraculous, for the curates, vicars, preachers, physicians, surgeons, and apothecaries who went to visit, treat, cure, preach, and administer to the sick all died of infection, whereas these cursed robbers and murderers never even took sick. How do you account for this, gentlemen? I ask you to think it over.

When the town had been plundered in this manner, they went on to the abbey, creating a horrible din. Finding it locked and barred, they split into two groups: the main body of the army marched on towards the Gué de Vède,[2] while seven companies of infantry and two hundred lancers stayed behind to break down the walls of the close and to lay waste the vineyards.

The monks, poor devils, did not know which saint to turn to. In their dilemma, they had the bells rung *ad capitulum capitulantes*.[3] It was decided here that they should form a solemn procession, with appropriate psalms and litanies *contra hostium insidias*,[4] with responses *pro pace*.[5]

There was in the abbey at this time a monk called

[1] **Seuilly** is located very close to the La Devinière and Rabelais may have gone to school at its abbey   [2] **Gué de Vède** a ford in a stream near La Devinière   [3] *ad . . . capitulantes* for calling the voting members of the community to the chapterhouse   [4] *contra . . . insidias* against the snares of the enemy   [5] *pro pace* for peace

Friar John Chopper, young, gay, spruce, good-natured, skillful, bold, adventurous, level-headed, tall, lean, with a good chin and a great nose, a crack dispatcher of prayers and masses, an expert at polishing off vigils—in short, a true monk if ever there was one since this monking world of ours first monked a monkery. A scholar to the teeth, moreover, when it came to the breviary.

Hearing the noise the enemy was making in the vineyard, Friar John went out to see what was going on. When he perceived that they were ravaging the close on which depended a whole year's drinking, he returned to the church choir, and there he found the other monks, struck dumb like so many bell-founders, chanting: *Ini, nim, pe, ne, ne, ne, ne, ne, ne, tum, ne, num, num, ini, i, mi, i, mi, co, o, ne, no, o, o, ne, no, ne, no, no, no, rum, ne, num, num.*[6] "That's a fine thing!" he said. "For God's sake, why don't you sing:

Farewell baskets, the vintage is in?

"The devil take me if they are not in our close, hacking down so many grapes and vines that, by God, there won't be any pickings there for four years to come. By St. James' belly, what will we poor devils drink in the meantime? Lord God, *da mihi potum!*"[7]

Then the prior of the cloister spoke up: "What is this drunkard doing here? Take him off to prison. Disturbing the divine service like this."

"But," protested Friar John, "what about the wine service? Let's be sure that it is not disturbed. You yourself, my Lord Prior, like to drink the best. So does every good man. A good man never despised good wine . . . that's a monastic apothegm. But, by God, the responses you're chanting here are out of season!

"Why are our devotions so short at harvest and at vintage time, and long in advent and all winter? The late

---

[6] *Ini . . . num Impetum inimicorum ne timueritis,* that is, fear not the onslaught of your enemies   [7] *da mihi potum* give me something to drink

Friar Macé Pelosse, of sainted memory, true zealot of our religion (or I'll be damned) said to me, I remember, that the reason was so that we might make and press our wine in the autumn, and drink it in the winter.

"Listen, gentlemen, all of you who like your wine, follow me, by Christ! May St. Anthony's fire burn me up if anyone drinks of the juice who has not defended the vines. God's body! the property of the Church! Ha, no, no, the devil! St. Thomas the Englishman[8] would have died for this. And if I die for it, won't I also be a saint like him? I won't die at it, however, for I'm going to do the killing."

So saying, he took off his long robe, and seized a staff of the cross, made of the heart of a sorb apple tree. Long as a lance, round, with a good grip, it was decorated after a fashion with fleurs-de-lis which had been almost all rubbed off. He sallied forth in a fine cassock, his cowl draped over it like a scarf, and he fell furiously on the enemy with his staff of the cross. Without order, standard, trumpet, or drum, they were in the process of despoiling the vineyard. The ensigns had laid their standards and colors against the wall, the drummers had caved in their drums and were filling them with grapes, the trumpets were full of vine branches, everyone was out of ranks. Friar John came down upon them so swiftly, without shouting a warning, that he bowled them over like pigs, slashing this way and that, in the good old-fashioned way.

He brained some, broke the arms and legs of others, unjointed the neck vertebrae of others, dislocated the loins of others still, bashed in their noses, gouged out their eyes, split their jaw bones, smashed in their teeth, crushed their shoulder blades, mangled their shins, unhinged their hips, and hewed to pieces the bones of their forearms and shanks. If any of them tried to hide in the thickest vines, Friar John broke their backbones and tore

[8] **St. Thomas the Englishman** Archbishop of Canterbury, better known as Thomas à Becket, who defended Church property against the King

them up like dogs. If any tried to save themselves by flight, he stove in their heads at the lambdoid suture. If any climbed a tree, thinking to find safety there, he impaled them through the guts with his staff. If any of his old acquaintances called to him: "Ho, Friar John, my friend, Friar John, I surrender!" he would answer: "You have no choice in the matter . . . but just the same, I'm going to send your souls to all the devils!"

And then he would give them a few good cracks. If any were rash enough to attempt to offer resistance, Friar John gave them an exhibition of muscular strength as he bashed in their chests, piercing the mediastinum and the heart. Giving it to others under the ribs, he mauled their stomachs so severely that they died at once. Others he struck so hard on the navel that their guts poured out. Some he ran through the testicles, piercing their rump-guts. This was without doubt the most horrible spectacle you ever saw!

Some invoked St. Barbara, others St. George, others St. Touchmenot, others Our Lady of Cunault, of Loretto, of Good Tidings, of Lenou, of Rivière! Some called on St. James, some on the Holy Shroud of Chambéry (which burned up three months later, and not a shred of it was saved), others on St. Cadouin, others on St. John of Angely, St. Eutropius of Saintes, St. Mexme of Chinon, St. Martin of Candes, St. Cloud of Cinais, on the relics of Javarzy,[9] and on a thousand other good little saints.

Some died without speaking, others spoke without dying. Some died in speaking, others spoke in dying. Others cried out in a loud voice: "Confession! Confession! *Confiteor! Miserere! In manus!*"[10]

The cry of the wounded was so loud that the Prior of the abbey, with all his monks, came out. When they saw these poor dogs lying among the vines, wounded to the point of death, they confessed some of them. While the

[9] **St. Barbara . . . Javarzy** all these, with the exception of St. Touchmenot, actually exist.　[10] *Confiteor . . . manus* I confess. Pity. Into Thy hands.

priests were busy confessing, the younger monklings rushed up to Friar John and asked him what they might do to help out. He told them to go slit the throat of all those he had already felled. And so, they put their capes on the nearest arbor, and began to slit throats, finishing off those Friar John had already struck down. Can you guess what instruments they used? Those small bladed knives which little children use to scoop the kernel out of walnuts.

Meanwhile, staff of the cross in hand, Friar John went over to the breach the enemy had made. Some of the monklings carried colors and standards into their rooms to make into garters. And when those who had confessed themselves tried to leave by the breach, Friar John laid them low, shouting: "These have confessed and repented, and have received absolution. Off they go to heaven, straight as a sickle . . . or as the road to Faye." [11]

Thus it was that Friar John's prowess routed that part of the army which had invaded the close, to the number of thirteen thousand, six hundred twenty-two, not counting, of course, the women and children. Maugis the hermit never acquitted himself more valiantly with his pilgrim's staff against the Saracens (as recounted in the *Deeds of the Four Sons of Aymon*[12]) than this monk did against the enemy with a staff of the cross.

How Picrochole Stormed La Roche Clermault
and the Regrets and Reluctance Expressed
by Grandgousier at Undertaking a War

While Friar John was skirmishing in the manner we have described against the invaders of the close, Picrochole hastily crossed the Gué de Vède with his men, and stormed La Roche Clermault without meeting any resistance whatever. Since night had already fallen, he de-

[11] road to Faye a very crooked road, near Chinon   [12] *Deeds . . . Aymon* romance of chivalry, published about 1480

cided to take up quarters there with his army and rest from the effects of his furious choler.

In the morning, he took by storm the outer bastions and castle, fortified them thoroughly, and stocked them with the necessary munitions. It was his intention to take a stand there if attacked from any other quarter, for the position was strong by art, by nature, and by its situation.

Let us leave him there now and return to our good friend Gargantua who is in Paris, diligently absorbed in the study of letters and in athletic exercises, and to that fine old man Grandgousier, his father, who, after supper, sat warming his genitals before a great, clear, roaring fire and, while waiting for the chestnuts to roast, was writing on the hearth with the burnt end of a stick used for poking the fire and telling his wife and family delightful stories of days gone by.

One of the shepherds who was guarding his vines, named Pillot, arrived just then and told Grandgousier of the outrages and pillagings that Picrochole, King of Lerné, was causing in his lands and domains, how he had plundered, laid waste, and sacked the whole country with the exception of the close of Seuilly which Friar John Choppers had so nobly saved, and how Picrochole, at that very moment, was at La Roche Clermault which he and his men were fortifying in great haste.

"Alas, alas!" cried Grandgousier. "What is this, my good people? Am I dreaming, or are they telling me the truth? Picrochole, my old, old friend, bound to me by race and alliance, has he come to attack me? What goads him to do so? Who is inciting him? Who is driving him on? Who has advised him to do so? Oh! Oh! Oh! Oh! Oh! my God, my Saviour, help me, inspire me, advise me what to do! I protest, I swear to Thee (for I invoke Thy help) that I have never done anything to displease Picrochole, nor done any harm to his people, nor have I ever pillaged his lands. But, on the contrary, I have aided him with men, money, favor and advice, whenever I could be of service to him. If he has committed such outrages against me, it can only be at the instigation of the Evil One. Good God, Thou knowest my courage, for from Thee nothing can be concealed. If it is simply that he has suddenly gone mad, and if Thou hast sent him to me to restore him to his senses, do Thou, then, grant me both the strength and the wisdom to bring him once more under the yoke of Thy holy will.

"Oh! Oh! Oh! my good men, my friends, and my faithful servants, should I prevent you from helping me in this crisis? Alas, my old age desires nothing but rest, and I have never sought anything but peace during my whole life; but I realize that I must now put armor on my tired and feeble shoulders, and take the lance and mace in my trembling hands in order to succor and protect my unhappy subjects. This is only as it should be since it is by the fruit of their labor and the sweat of their brow that I, and my children, and household are sustained.

"Nevertheless, I shall not go to war until I have exhausted every possibility of peace—on that, I am determined."

Grandgousier summoned his council then and laid the matter before them. They decided to send some prudent man to Picrochole to inquire why he had suddenly broken the peace and invaded lands to which he had not the slightest claim. They resolved, in addition, to summon Gargantua and his men to the protection and defence of the country in its hour of need. These decisions were approved by Grandgousier, and he ordered that they be carried out. Accordingly, within the hour, he sent his lackey Basque to find Gargantua as quickly as possible and to give him the following letter.

THE TENOR OF THE LETTER WHICH GRANDGOUSIER WROTE TO GARGANTUA

The enthusiasm with which you are pursuing your studies would deter me from interrupting you in your philosophical leisure were it not for the fact that the security of my old age has been imperiled by friends and allies in whom I had confidence. But, since it is my irrevocable destiny to be troubled by those on whom I have relied most, I find myself forced to summon you back to the defence of the people and property which are yours by natural right. For, just as arms are weak abroad if there is no counsel at home, so study is vain and consultation useless unless applied fittingly and appropriately.

My intention is not to provoke, but to appease; not to attack, but to defend; not to conquer, but to protect my faithful subjects and hereditary lands which Picrochole has invaded without cause or occasion. And he is continuing his mad enterprise, committing excesses which are intolerable to any freeborn man.

I have assumed the duty of moderating his tyrannical choler, offering him anything I thought might satisfy him. On several occasions, I have sent friendly envoys to inquire in what, by whom, and how he felt himself wronged. But his sole reply has been of wilful defiance coupled with the statement that the only right that he claimed in my lands was his own pleasure. From this, I realized that God Almighty had abandoned him to the rule of his own free will and senses, both of which are worthless if not directed constantly by Divine Grace. And so, I cannot help but feel that God has sent him here to me, with hostile standards, so that I might put him in his place and bring him back to his senses.

Therefore, my dear son, as soon as you have read this letter, come home as quickly as you can, not so much to help me (this is mere filial duty), but your own people, whom reason orders you to protect and preserve. The whole thing must be done with the least bloodshed possible and, if it can be managed, by expediency, policy, and strategy, we shall save every soul of them and send them all back happy to their homes.

My dearest son, may the peace of Christ, our Redeemer,

be with you. My greetings to Ponocrates, Gymnastes, and Eudemon.

The twentieth of September.
Your father,
Grandgousier.

How Certain of Picrochole's Officers Put him in Extreme Peril by their Rash Advice

After the cakes had been taken, the Duke of Riffraff, Count Swashbuckler, and Captain Krapp appeared before Picrochole and said to him:

"Sire, today we are going to make you the happiest, most chivalrous prince that ever was since the death of Alexander of Macedon."

"Put on your hats, my lords, put on your hats," [1] said Picrochole.

"Many thanks," they said. "Sire, we have come to do our duty, and this is what we suggest: that you leave a captain here with a garrison strong enough to hold the place—it seems quite safe both by natural situation and by reason of the fortifications you have erected—and that you divide your army in two, as you could very well do. One part of it will fall upon Grandgousier and his men and will defeat him in the very first skirmish. There you'll obtain lots of money, for the villein[2] is rolling in it. Villein, we say, for what noble prince ever had a cent? To hoard money is the work of a villein.

"The other part, in the meanwhile, will march on Aunis, Saintonge, Angoumois, and Gascony, as well as Périgord, Médoc, and Landes.[3] Without the least resistance, they will capture cities, castles, and fortresses. At Bayonne, Saint Jean-de-Luz, and Fuerterrabia[4] you will seize all the ships and coast down toward Galicia[5] and

---

[1] hats were removed in the presence of the King   [2] villein member of a class of serfs in the feudal system   [3] Aunis . . . Landes provinces extending south through France to the Spanish border   [4] Bayonne . . . Fuerterrabia towns near or on the Spanish border   [5] Galicia province in the NW corner of Spain

Portugal, plundering all the seaports along the way as far as Lisbon, where you will find all the reinforcements you might require. God help us! and Spain will surrender, since the Spaniards are a race of louts. Passing the Straits of Seville, you will erect two columns more magnificent than those of Hercules, to the perpetual memory of your name. These straits shall be called the Picrocholine Sea. Once the Picrocholine Sea is crossed, here's Barbarossa[6] who makes himself your slave . . ."

"I'll show him mercy," said Picrochole.

"That's fine," they said, "providing he's willing to be baptized. And you will attack the kingdoms of Tunis, Bizerta, Algiers, Bône, Cyrene, and all Barbary.[7] Your next step will be to take possession of Majorca, Minorca, Sardinia, Corsica, and the other islands of the Ligurean and Balearic Sea. Going along the coast to the left, you conquer all of Narbonnais Gaul,[8] Provence, the land of the Allobroges,[9] Genoa, Florence, Lucca, and, by God, Rome! The poor Mr. Pope, he's already dead from fright!"

"I swear," said Picrochole, "I'll never kiss his slipper."

"Once you've taken Italy, there's Naples, Calabria, Apulia,[10] and Sicily to be sacked, along with Malta. I only hope that those ridiculous knights, formerly of Rhodes,[11] try to resist so we can see the color of their urine!"

"I shouldn't mind going to Loretto," [12] said Picrochole.

"No, no," they said, "that will be for the way back. Next you will take Candia, Cyprus, Rhodes, and the Cyclades,[13] and then you will swoop down on Morea.[14]

[6] **Barbarossa** name given two brothers, pirates and masters of Algiers in the early 16th century   [7] **Tunis . . . Bône** towns of Cyrene and Barbary, on the western Mediterranean coast of Africa   [8] **Narbonnais Gaul** Mediterranean coast of France around Narbonne   [9] **Allobroges** lived in the province of Savoy   [10] **Calabria** and **Apulia** are two of the southernmost provinces on the Italian peninsula   [11] **The Knights of St. John** of Jerusalem, driven from Rhodes by the Turks in 1522, went to Malta in 1530   [12] **Loretto** on the Adriatic coast of Italy, site of a famous pilgrimage   [13] **Candia . . . Cyclades** islands in the Aegean   [14] **Morea** the Peloponnesos

No sooner said than done. By St. Ninny, God help Jerusalem! The Sultan doesn't stand a chance against you!"

"I," said Picrochole, "will rebuild the Temple of Solomon."

"Not yet," said they, "wait a bit. Never be too hasty in your undertakings. Remember what Octavius Augustus said: *Festina lente.*[15] First you should take Asia Minor, Caria, Lycia, Pamphilia, Cilicia, Lydia, Phrygia, Mysia, Bithynia, Carrasia, Adalia, Samagaria, Kastamuni, Luga, Sebasta,[16] and everything up to the Euphrates."

"Shall we see Babylon and Mount Sinai?"

"There's no need of that at this time," they said to him. "Isn't it enough to have crossed the Hircanian Sea,[17] and to have straddled the two Armenias and the three Arabias?" [18]

"Good God!" said he, "we're out of our minds! We're really done for!"

"What's the matter?" they asked.

"What are we going to drink in the desert? Didn't Julian Augustus and his whole army die there of thirst?" [19]

"We have already taken care of everything," they said. "You have nine thousand fourteen huge ships in the Syrian Sea, loaded down with the best wine in the world. I see them sailing into Jaffa.[20] There will be twenty-two hundred thousand camels and sixteen hundred elephants which you will have taken in a hunt near Sidjilmassa,[21] when you entered Libya. Besides, there's the whole caravan which goes to Mecca. Surely that will be wine enough!"

"Yes, of course," said he, "but it isn't fresh!"

"Gods and little fishes," said they, "a brave man, a

[15] *Festina lente* make haste slowly [16] **Caria . . . Sebasta** countries and towns in Asia Minor [17] **Hircanian Sea** the Caspian Sea [18] **two Armenias** Great and Little Armenia; **three Arabias** Arabia Deserta, Arabia Felix, Arabia Petraea as the Ancients divided the country [19] **Julian** the Apostate died in a campaign against the Persians and his army was decimated in the desert from heat and thirst [20] **Jaffa** port in Israel [21] **Sidjilmassa** city in Morocco

conqueror, one who pretends and aspires to the empire of the universe, cannot always have things as he wants. Thank God that you and your army have arrived safe and sound at the Tigris."

"But," he inquired, "what's the other part of my army doing all this time, the part which defeated Grand-gousier?"

"They've not been asleep," they replied. "We'll join them soon. They have taken Brittany for you, Normandy, Flanders, Hainaut, Brabant, Artois, Holland, and Zee-land.[22] They have crossed the Rhine on the bellies of the Swiss and the Germans, and a detachment has conquered Luxembourg, Lorraine, Champagne, and Savoy as far as Lyons. There they are meeting your forces returning from the naval conquest of the Mediterranean Sea, and they reassemble in Bohemia after having sacked Swabia, Würtemburg, Bavaria, Austria, Moravia, and Styria.[23] Then they descend upon Lübeck, Norway, Sweden, Denmark, Gothland, Greenland, and the Hanse-atics[24] as far as the Arctic Sea. Now they capture the Orkney Islands and subjugate Scotland, England, and Ireland. From there, sailing by the Sandy Sea and Sar-matia, they defeat and conquer Prussia, Poland, Lithuania, Russia, Wallachia, Transylvania, and Hungary, Bulgaria, Turkey, and now they are in Constantinople."

"Let's go join them as quickly as possible," said Picro-chole, "for I want to be emperor of Trebizond [25] as well. Are we not going to slaughter all those Turkish and Mohammedan dogs?"

"What the devil do you think we'll do?" they said. "And you will give their lands and possessions to those who have served you faithfully."

"That's only reasonable," said he, "that's only just. You may have Carmania,[26] Syria, and all Palestine."

---

[22] **Normandy . . . Zeeland** French, Belgium and Dutch provinces   [23] **Styria** Austrian province   [24] **Hanseatics** German Baltic cities   [25] **Trebizond** Moslem city in Asia Minor   [26] **Carmania** Asian Turkey

"Ha! Sire," they said, "that's most kind of you. Many thanks and may God ever make you prosper."

Now there happened to be, among those present, an old gentleman, experienced in undertakings of various sorts, a true veteran warrior by the name of Echephron.[27] Upon hearing these remarks, he said:

"I'm very much afraid that this project will be like the farce of the pot of milk and the cobbler who dreamed that he was rich. Then, when the pot broke, he had no dinner. What do you expect to get from all these great conquests? What will be the outcome of so much toil and travail?"

"The result," said Picrochole, "will be that, when we get back, we will enjoy our leisure."

"And suppose you never get back?" Echephron said. "The journey is long and dangerous. Would it not be better for you to enjoy your leisure right now without exposing us to all these dangers?"

"Oh!" said Swashbuckler, "here's a fine dreamer! Are we supposed to hide in the chimney corner and spend the rest of our lives stringing pearls with the ladies or knitting like Sardanapalus?[28] Nothing ventured, nothing gained— not even a horse or mule, says Solomon."

"He who ventures too much," Echephron said, "loses both horse and mule, Malcon answered."[29]

"Enough!" Picrochole exclaimed, "let us proceed. I fear nothing except those devilish legions of Grandgousier. What would we do if, while we are in Mesopotamia, they should fall upon our rear?"

"We can take care of that," said Krapp. "A little mission which you'll send to the Muscovites will bring you immediately four hundred fifty thousand picked soldiers. If you would only appoint me your lieutenant, I'd kill a

[27] **Echephron** name meaning Prudent   [28] **Sardanapalus** luxurious Assyrian potentate   [29] the allusion is to the *Dialogues of Salomon and Malcon* (15th century); Malcon represents common sense and Solomon wisdom

feather for its birds.[30] I roar, I grit my teeth, I fall upon the enemy, I strike, I capture, I kill!"

"Forward," shouted Picrochole. "Make haste! And let him that loves me follow me!"

How Gargantua Had the Abbey of Thélème built for the Monk

There remained only the monk to provide for.[1] Gargantua wanted to make him abbot of Seuilly, but Friar John refused. He tried to give him the Abbey of Bourgueil or of Saint Florent, whichever would suit him better, or both if he wanted; but the monk answered flatly that he wanted nothing to do with the charge or government of monks.

"For," he explained, "how shall I govern others when I am unable to govern myself? If you are of the opinion that I have done you, and can in the future do you good service, let me found an abbey after my own plan."

This request pleased Gargantua, and he offered his lands of Thélème, by the Loire, two leagues from the great forest of Port Huault.[2] The monk then asked Gargantua to found a religious order contrary to all others.

"First then," said Gargantua, "you must not build a wall around it, for all other abbeys are stoutly enclosed."

"So they are," said the monk, "and not without cause, for where there are *murs,* walls, before, and *murs,* walls, behind, there are many *murmures,*[3] murmurs, envy, and plotting."

Moreover, seeing that in certain abbeys in this world, there is a rule that if any woman enter in (I mean honest and chaste ones), the ground they walk on must be washed, it was decreed that if any monk or nun should

[30] **feather for its birds** in his excitement he says the opposite of what he means   [1] Gargantua has already rewarded the other heroes of the Picrocholine War   [2] **Port Huault** near Chinon   [3] *murmures* play on words of the kind Rabelais likes

happen to enter this new abbey, every place they set foot would have to be thoroughly cleansed. And because in other monasteries and convents everything is run, fixed, and regulated by hours, it was decreed that there would be no clock or dial whatsoever at Thélème, but that all work would be done as the occasion or opportunity might arise. For, Gargantua said, the greatest waste of time he knew was to count hours. What good came of it? And the greatest stupidity in the world was regulating one's life by the sound of a bell instead of by reason and common sense.

Besides, since in those days women were not put into convents unless they were blind in one eye, lame, hunch-backed, ugly, misshapen, crazy, silly, deformed, disreputable, nor men unless they were cankered, ill-bred dunces or just plain trouble-makers . . .

"By the way," asked Friar John, "if a women is neither beautiful nor good, what's she good for?"

"To put into a convent," replied Gargantua.

"Yes," added the monk, "and to make shirts."

. . . it was decided that they would admit only beautiful, shapely women, pleasing of form and nature, and handsome, athletic, and personable men.

Again, because men entered the convents of women only by stealth and clandestinely, it was decreed that there would be no women there unless there were also men, nor men unless there were women.

Moreover, since both men as well as women, once they have been received into the religious life and had spent one year in the novitiate, were forced to remain there for the rest of their lives, it was decided that men as well as women would be able to leave Thélème whenever they wished and without restrictions of any sort.

Furthermore, since members of a religious community usually take three vows—namely, chastity, poverty and obedience—it was decreed that in this abbey one might honorably marry, enjoy wealth, and live in perfect freedom.

As for the entrance age, it was stipulated that women

were to be admissible between the ages of ten and fifteen, men between twelve and eighteen.

How the Abbey of the Thelemites was Built and Endowed

To build and furnish the abbey, Gargantua gave twenty-seven hundred thousand eight hundred and thirty-one gold crowns. And yearly, until everything was completed, he undertook to give sixteen hundred and sixty-nine thousand crowns with the sun imprint, and as many with the seven stars imprint, the whole to be paid from the toll receipts of the Dive River.[1] For the foundation and support of the abbey, he gave in perpetuity two million three hundred sixty-nine thousand five hundred fourteen nobles with the rose imprint, free of all tax and encumbrances, payable yearly at the abbey gate. These privileges were all corroborated by letters patent.

The building was hexagonal, and at each corner rose a great round tower sixty yards in diameter, each identical in size and appearance. The river Loire flowed past the north tower, which was called *Arctice*.[2] East of it was *Calaer*,[3] then, successively, *Anatole*,[4] *Mesembrine*,[5] *Hesperia*,[6] and finally, *Cryere*.[7] The distance between each tower was three hundred and twelve yards. The building had six stories, counting the underground cellars as one. The second story was vaulted like a basket handle; the others were faced in Flanders gypsum,[8] with pendants. The roof was covered with fine slate, lined with lead, and adorned with little statues of men and animals, all nicely matched and gilt. The gutters jutted out from the walls, between the casement arches, and were painted with diagonal gold and blue figures. They ran down to the

---

[1] **Dive River** is actually a small stream near Chinon, not navigable at this point [2] **Arctice** Northern [3] **Calaer** means situated in the balmy air [4] **Anatole** means Eastern [5] **Mesembrine** means Southern [6] **Hesperia** means Occidental [7] **Cryere** means Glacial [8] **Flanders gypsum** is a kind of plaster

ground and emptied into huge pipes which carried the water into the river below.

This building was a hundred times more magnificent than Bonnivet, Chambord, or Chantilly,[9] and it contained nine thousand three hundred and thirty-two suites, each one with a dressing-room, a study, a wardrobe, an oratory, and an exit which led to a great hall. Between each tower, in the center of the main building, was a spiral stairway. Its steps were partly of porphyry, partly of Numidian stone, and partly of serpentine marble. Each one was twenty-two feet long and three fingers thick, and there were twelve of them between landings. At each landing there were two fine antique arches which let in the light, and through these one could enter a loggia of the same width as the stairs. The stairway ran up to the roof and ended in a pavilion.[10] There was a great hallway on either side of the stairs, and the suites were off the hallways.

In the wing between the *Arctice* and *Cryere* towers were rich libraries of Greek, Latin, Hebrew, French, Tuscan and Spanish works, arranged on different levels according to language. There was another marvelous stairway in the middle of the building. Its entrance, which was outside, consisted of an arch thirty-six feet wide. This stair was so well proportioned and so capacious that six soldiers, with their lances at rest, could ride up it abreast as far as the roof.[11] Between *Anatole* and *Mesembrine* were large and splendid galleries covered with murals representing heroic feats of old, scenes from history, and geographical scenes. Here was still another stairway and gate similar to those we saw on the river side . . .

[9] **Bonnivet . . . Chantilly** three of the most magnificent castles of the day [10] There is a staircase in the castle of Chambord similar to this one [11] There is such a staircase in the castle of Amboise

Description of the Thelemite Manor

In the middle of the lower court stood a magnificent fountain made of beautiful alabaster, and surmounted by the Three Graces with cornucopias spouting water through their breasts, mouths, ears, eyes, and other orifices.

That part of the building which faced this court rested upon great pillars of chalcedony and of porphory. It had beautiful Roman arches under which were lovely galleries, long and wide, adorned with paintings and trophies of various animals: the horns of deer, unicorns, rhinoceroses, hippopotami, elephants' tusks, and other curious and interesting objects.

The quarters for the ladies ran from the *Arctice* to the *Mesembrine*. The men occupied the rest. Facing the quarters for the ladies, between the first two towers, were the recreational facilities: the tilting yard, the riding school, the theater, and the natatorium with wonderful pools on three different levels, furnished with all the necessary equipment and with a bountiful supply of myrtle water.

There was a beautiful pleasure garden near the river with, in the middle, a fine labyrinth. The handball courts and football fields were between the two other towers. Near *Cryere* was the orchard full of fruit trees of every kind, all set out in quincunxes.[1] Beyond was the great park, abounding in savage beasts of every sort.

The space between the third pair of towers was set aside for the shooting ranges: here were targets for harquebus, long bow, and crossbow. The servants' quarters were opposite *Hesperia*, and they were one story high. Beyond the servants' quarters were the stables. The falconry was beyond this, and it was managed by expert falconers, and supplied annually by the Cretans, the Venetians, and the Sarmatians with all kinds of out-of-the-ordinary birds:

---

[1] quincunxes one at each corner of a square, and one in the center

eagles, gerfalcons, goshawks, sakers, lanners, falcons, sparrow hawks, merlins, and others, all so well trained and domesticated that when they flew afield for their own sport they never failed to catch every bird they encountered. The hunting lodge was a little farther off, towards the park.

All the halls, rooms, and chambers were tapestried in various ways, and this was changed according to the seasons of the year. The floors were covered with green cloth, and the beds were all embroidered. There was a crystal mirror set in a heavy gold frame adorned with pearls in each dressing room, and it was of such a size that you could see all of yourself in it at once. Near the exit of the ladies' halls were the perfumers and the hairdressers who ministered to the men who came to visit the ladies. These attendants supplied the ladies' rooms with rose water each morning, orange-flower water and angelica; and in each room a precious atomizer gave forth all sorts of aromatic drugs.

How the Monks and Nuns of Thélème were Dressed

The ladies, when the abbey was first founded, dressed as they pleased and felt. Subsequently, of their own free will, they introduced the following reform.

They wore scarlet or kermes-red stockings which reached some three inches above the knee, and the borders were exquisitely embroidered and slashed. Their garters were of the same colors as their bracelets, and clasped the leg both above and below the knee. Their shoes, pumps, and slippers were made of brilliant velvet, red or violet, and were shaped in the form of a lobster's barbel.

Over their slips, they wore a fine bodice of silk camlet material, and over that a taffeta petticoat, white, red, beige, grey, etc. Above this went a skirt of silver taffeta, with fine gold embroidery and delicate cross-stitch work. According to the wearer's whim or the season of the year, these skirts might be of satin, damask, orange velvet, beige, green, ash-grey, blue, bright yellow, brilliant red, white, cloth-of-gold, cloth-of-silver, of brocaded or of embroidered work in keeping with the feast days.

Their gowns, according to the season, were of cloth-of-gold with silver embossing, or red satin with gold brocade, or of white, blue, black or beige taffeta, silk serge, silk camlet, velvet, cloth-of-silver, cloth-of-gold, or of velvet or satin with gold facings of varying designs.

In summer, on certain days, instead of gowns, they wore cloaks of the above mentioned materials, or sleeveless jackets cut in the Moorish fashion and made of violet-colored velvet, with raised gold stitching over silver purl, or with gold piping and cording, with small Indian pearls at their ends. And they always wore a fine plume, of the same color as their sleeves, and well trimmed with golden spangles. In winter, they wore taffeta gowns of the colors already mentioned, trimmed with the fur of lynxes, black-spotted weasels, Calabrian martens, sable, and other rare skins.

Their beads, rings, chains, and necklaces were of precious stones: carbuncles, rubies, balas rubies, diamonds, sapphires, emeralds, turquoises, garnets, agates, beryls, and pearls both great and small.

They fixed their hair according to the season. In winter, it was in the French fashion; in spring, in the Spanish; in summer, in the Tuscan. On Sundays and holidays, however, they wore it in the French fashion, which is more seemly and modest.

The men were dressed according to their own taste. Their hose were of light wool or serge cloth, scarlet, kermes-red, white, or black. Their velvet breeches were of the same colors, or very nearly so, and they were embroidered and slashed to suit their fancy. Their doublets were of cloth-of-gold, cloth-of-silver, velvet, satin, damask, or taffeta, of the same shades, slashed, embroidered, and fitted in a most excellent fashion. Their points were of matching silk, and their buckles of well-enamelled gold.

Their cloaks and jerkins were of cloth-of-gold, gold tissue, cloth-of-silver, or velvet. Their over-garments were as costly as those worn by the ladies. Their girdles were of silk, of the same color as the doublet. Each one had a fine sword at his side, with gilt handle, a velvet scabbard of the same color as the breeches, and the ferrule[1] was a wondrous example of the goldsmith's art. The dagger was the same. Their caps were of black velvet, trimmed with a great many beads and gold buttons, with a white plume set in jauntily, parted by golden spangles, and hung with splendid rubies, emeralds, etc.

Such was the sympathy between the men and women that they dressed in a similar fashion every day. And in order to be sure of it, certain gentlemen were appointed to inform the men every morning what garments the ladies planned to wear that particular day, for everything was done as the ladies wished.

Handsome though the clothes were and rich the accoutrements, neither men nor women lost any time whatsoever in getting dressed. The wardrobe masters had all the clothing ready each morning, and the maids were so well instructed that they had their mistresses dressed from head to foot in no time at all. To facilitate matters, near the woods of Thélème, there was a row of cottages over a distance of half a league, well lighted and equipped, which housed the goldsmiths, lapidaries, embroiderers, tailors, gold thread workers, velvet makers, tapestry makers, and upholsterers. Here each worked at his trade, and everything they produced went to the monks and nuns. These workmen were supplied with materials and cloth by my Lord Nausicletus[2] who, every year, sent seven ships from the Pearl and Cannibal Islands, laden with ingots of gold, raw silk, pearls, and precious stones. If any of the pearls showed signs of age or loss of native luster, the

[1] ferrule the handle guard [2] Nausicletus name, meaning renowned for his ships, given by Homer in the Odyssey to the Pheacians

workmen restored them by feeding them to roosters, much as one gives a purge to falcons.[3]

How the Thelemites were Governed in their Manner of Living

Their whole life was regulated not by laws, statutes or rules, but according to their own free will and choice. They arose when they pleased, drank, ate, worked, slept when the spirit moved them. No one awoke them, no one forced them to eat or drink, or do anything at all. For this was the way it was established by Gargantua. There was only this one clause in their rule:

DO AS THOU WILT[1]

because men who are free, well born, well bred, at home in society, possess a natural instinct and drive which impels them to virtuous deeds, and which restrains them from vice, and they called this instinct honor. Whenever they find themselves depressed or enslaved by subjection or constraint—because we all long for forbidden things and desire things which are denied us—they apply their noble inclination to virtue so as to shake off the yoke of servitude.

In the enjoyment of their liberty, they entered into a laudable emulation in doing, all of them, anything which was pleasing to any one of them. If someone, man or woman, said: "Let us drink," they all drank. If someone said: "Let us go play in the fields," they all went. When hawking or hunting were in order, the ladies went mounted upon beautiful hackneys or proud-stepping palfreys, a sparrow hawk, a lanner, or a merlin on one daintily gloved wrist, while the men bore other kinds of birds.

They were so nobly educated that there was not a single man or woman among them who did not know

[3] this method of restoring pearls was suggested by Averroes, famous Arabic philosopher and physician [1] **Do . . . Wilt** the word Thélème itself means Free Will

how to read, write, sing, play a musical instrument, speak five or six languages, and compose in any one of them both poetry and prose. There never were seen knights so bold, so gallant, so adroit on foot and on horse, so athletic, so alert, so adept at handling weapons of every kind. There never were seen ladies so proper, so dainty, so comely, more deft at handwork and needlework, more frank and free in every feminine art.

And thus, when it came time for any member to leave the abbey, either at the request of his parents or for some other reason, he took with him one of the ladies—the one who had chosen him for her devoted follower—and they were married. And if they had lived in devotion and friendship at Thélème, they tended to find even more of both in marriage; and they continued to love one another to the end of their lives as much as they did on the day of their wedding . . .[2]

[2] The life of the Thelemites recalls that of certain Italian courts as depicted by Castiglione in his *Il Cortegiano* (1528)

THE SECOND BOOK

❦

Pantagruel
King of the Dipsodes
Restored to his True Nature together
with his Deeds and Horrendous Feats

SET DOWN BY THE LATE
MONSIEUR ALCOFRIBAS
ABSTRACTOR OF QUINTESSENCE

THE AUTHOR'S PROLOGUE

Most illustrious and most chivalrous champions, gentlemen, and others who do not hesitate to indulge in amuse-
ments and honest entertainment, you have recently seen,
read, and known the *Great and Inestimable Chronicles of
the Enormous Giant Gargantua*,[1] and, like faithful souls,
you have believed them gallantly, and have often spent
your time with honorable ladies and young girls, when
you were out of conversation, telling fine long stories from
them, for all of which you deserve vast praise and sempiternal memory.

It is my wish that every reader lay aside what he has
to do, give up all thought of his own profession, forget
all about his own affairs, in order to concentrate his
attention exclusively upon my tales, his mind neither
distracted nor elsewhere, until he has learned them by
heart. If ever the art of printing should be lost, or if all
books should perish, each and every one of you would
then be able to teach them to future generations, to pass

[1] *Great . . . Gargantua* anonymous tale which may have inspired Rabelais to compose the present work

71

them on from mouth to mouth to his successors and survivors, like a secret religious doctrine. For there is greater profit in them than a motley lot of poxed critics would have you believe, who understand these little drolleries even less than Rachet[2] the *Institutes*.[3]

I have known a number of high and mighty lords who, while hunting huge beasts, or flying falcons after wild ducks, if it so happened that the animal was not tracked down or that the falcon refused to soar in pursuit, were most irritated, as is quite natural, when they saw their prey escaping; but they found refuge and comfort, and a way out of their exasperation by repeating the inestimable exploits of the said Gargantua.

There are people in the world (this is no joke) who, when suffering greatly from toothache, after spending their fortune on physicians to no avail, have found no more expedient remedy than the said *Chronicles* placed between two pieces of warm linen and applied to the sore spot, with a little quickshit powder, as a poultice.

What shall I say of those wretched poxed and gouty devils? How often have we seen them covered with ointment and grease, their faces glistening like a larder keyhole, their teeth chattering in their heads like an organ or spinet keyboard when it is played upon, and their throats foaming like a boar's at bay when chased by a pack of bloodhounds into a net! What did they do then? Their sole consolation was to have someone read to them a few pages from said book. And I have seen some who would give themselves to five score giant casks of devils if they did not obtain manifest relief from the reading of this book while they were being held in limbo,[4] in much the same way as women in childbirth do when someone reads to them from the *Life of St. Margaret*.

Is that nothing at all? Show me a book, in any language,

[2] **Rachet** celebrated professor of Law at Dôle [3] *Institutes* Roman law as codified by Justinian [4] **limbo** between Heaven and Hell; here refers to the steam bath used at the time in the treatment of syphilis

in any branch of art or science whatsoever, which has such virtues, properties, and prerogatives, and I will buy you a pint of tripe. No, gentlemen, no! It is peerless, incomparable, and unprecedented. I maintain it as far as the fire *exclusive*.[5] And if anyone maintains the opposite, let him be denounced as a false prophet, a champion of predestination,[6] an imposter, and a seducer.

It is true that you can find certain occult properties in some books of fine quality such as *Downbottle, Orlando Furioso, Robert the Devil, Fierabras, William the Fearless, Huon of Bordeaux, Mandeville,* and *Matabrune;*[7] but there is absolutely no comparison between them and the book we are talking about. The whole world has realized from infallible experience the great advantages and benefits which accrue from the said Gargantuan *Chronicles.* Why, within two months the printers sold more copies of it than they will Bibles for nine years to come.

Desiring, therefore, to increase your amusement even more, I, your humble servant, offer you here another book of the same stamp—except that it is a bit more worthy of belief and respect than its predecessor. Do not imagine (unless you want to go astray on purpose) that I speak of my book as the Jews speak of the Law.[8] I was not born under such a star, and I never lie or make false representation. I speak of it like a lusty votary, I mean notary, of martyred lovers, and noter of affections:[9] *Quod vidimus testamur.*[10] Here you have the horrendous deeds and prowesses of Pantagruel, whom I have served from infancy until now, and by whose leave I have come to visit my native cow-country to see if any of my relatives are still alive.

But to put an end to this prologue, may I deliver my-

---

[5] *exclusive* until menaced by burning at the stake, exclusively [6] these remarks are directed at Calvin and his followers [7] *Downbottle* and *Matabrune* are facetious titles [8] Law in ignorance, that is [9] laborious reference to Papal notaries who drafted the Acts of the Martyrs and who had a reputation for lechery [10] *Quod . . . testamur* We attest to what we have seen

self up, body and soul, to a hundred thousand basketfuls
of fine devils if I have lied even once in this whole story.
By the same token, may St. Anthony burn you with his
fire, may epilepsy floor you, may lightning, ulcers and
chancres cripple you

> May the fine fire of purulent pox,
> Fine as hair from an old cow's locks
> Covered with quicksilver, by my soul,
> Run straight up your old bunghole,

and may you fall into a pit of brimstone and fire, like
Sodom and Gomorrah, if you do not believe steadfastly
everything that I am about to relate in the present
Chronicle!

ON THE NATIVITY OF THE MOST
REDOUBTABLE PANTAGRUEL

Gargantua, at the age of four hundred and forty-four,
begot his son Pantagruel, with his wife Badebec, daughter
of the King of the Amaurotes[1] in Utopia.[2] She died in
childbirth, for Pantagruel was so marvelously big and
heavy that he could not come to light without suffocating
his mother.

But in order to understand fully the cause and reason
of the name which was given him in baptism, you must
remember that there was so great a drought that year
throughout all Africa that for thirty-six months, three
weeks and four days, thirteen hours and a bit longer, there
was not a drop of rain, and the heat from the sun was so
fierce that the whole earth was parched. It was no hotter
even in the days of Elijah[3] than it was then, for there
was not a single tree on earth that had either leaf or
flower. The grass had lost its greenness, and rivers and
fountains ran dry. The poor fish, abandoned by their
element, crawled about on solid ground, crying and scream-

---

[1] **Amaurotes** means Difficult to see   [2] **Utopia** St. Thomas More's
Utopia was published in 1516   [3] **Elijah** during which time
there was a three year drought over the land

ing most horribly. Birds fell from the air for want of moisture; wolves, foxes, deer, wild boars, does, hares, rabbits, weasels, martens, badgers, and other animals were found dead in the fields, their mouths agape. As for human beings, their state was very sad. You should have seen them with their tongues hanging out like a hound's after a six-hour run. Some threw themselves into wells. Others lay under a cow's belly in order to be in the shade— Homer calls these the *Alibantes*.[4] The whole country was at a standstill. It was a pitiable sight to see how men toiled to escape from this horrible alteration. Great efforts were required to keep the holy water in the churches from being used up; instructions were given by my Lords the Cardinals and the Holy Father that no one should be permitted to take more than one lick of it. And so, whenever you went into church, you could see scores of unhappy, parched wretches trailing after the person who distributed the water, their jaws open for one tiny little drop, like the wicked rich man,[5] so that none of it would be lost. Ah! fortunate was he who had a cool well-stocked wine cellar that year.

A philosopher, raising the question why sea water is salty, relates that when Phoebus[6] gave the reins of his luminous chariot to his son Phaëton, the said Phaëton, unskilled in the art of following the ecliptic lines between the two tropics of the sun's sphere, strayed from his path and got so close to the earth that he dried up all the countries underneath. He burned as well that part of the sky which philosophers call the *Via Lactea*,[7] and good drinkers St. James' Way,[8] although the cleverest of the poets declare that this is the spot where Juno's milk fell when she suckled Hercules. And the earth was so heated that it broke into an enormous sweat, and it sweated out

[4] *Alibantes* means the Desiccated [5] wicked rich man who asked from Hell that Lazarus dip the tip of his finger in water to cool his tongue [6] Phoebus is the god of the sun [7] *Via Lactea* the Milky Way [8] St. James' Way because it pointed the way to St. James of Compostella

the whole sea, making it salty, since all sweat is salty. You can verify this if you taste your own or that of your pox-stricken friends when they are made to perspire,[9] either way is fine by me.

Just about the same thing happened the year I am speaking of. One Friday, when everybody was rapt in devotions, and a fine procession with plenty of litanies and splendid sermons had been organized to beseech Almighty God to cast a merciful eye upon them in their affliction, drops of water suddenly began to appear quite clearly on the ground, exactly as on a person sweating copiously. And these poor people began to rejoice as if this were a great blessing. Some said that there was not a drop of moisture in the air for rain, and that the earth was making up for the deficiency. Others claimed that this was the rain of the Antipodes, as described by Seneca in his *Quaestionum naturalium*, Book IV [10], when he talks about the origin and source of the Nile. But they were mistaken. For when the procession was over and they tried to gather up this dew and drink it down, they discovered that it was only brine, far saltier than the saltiest water of the sea.

And because he was born on this very day, Gargantua called his son Pantagruel; for *Panta* means All in Greek, and *Gruel* means Athirst in Saracen,[11] the inference being that the whole world was athirst at the hour of his birth. Moreover, his father realized prophetically that one day his son would become Lord of the Thirsty, a fact indicated even more surely by a further portent. For while his mother Badebec was bringing him forth, and as the midwives were preparing to receive him, there issued first from her belly seventy-eight salt-vendors, each leading a salt-laden mule by the halter. They were followed by nine dromedaries loaded with ham and smoked ox tongues, seven camels charged with salted eels, and, finally, twenty-five cartloads

---

[9] Usual treatment for syphilis at the time [10] the reference is doubtful [11] Facetious etymology: Pantagruel is actually a demon in French medieval plays; he made everyone he came in contact with thirsty

of leeks, garlic, onions, scallions. This terrified the midwives, but some of them said:

"This is a good provision! As it is we drink sluggishly, not vigorously. This must be a good omen since these are foods which make one thirsty!"

As they rattled on in this way, out came Pantagruel, as hairy as a bear. This prompted one of the women to prophesy:

"He is born with hair, and will accomplish wondrous things. And if he lives, he will grow older."

Gargantua's Mourning at the Death of his Wife Badebec

When Pantagruel was born, who do you think was really amazed and perplexed? Gargantua, his father. For seeing, on the one hand, his wife Badebec dead, and, on the other hand, his son Pantagruel born, so handsome and so big, he did not know what to say or do. The doubt which troubled his mind was whether he should weep over the death of his wife or laugh over the birth of his son. There were sophistical arguments on either hand which gagged him. He could frame them all very well *in modo et figura*,[1] but he was unable to resolve them. And so he floundered like a mouse caught in a trap, or a kite[2] in a snare.

"Shall I weep?" he cried. "Yes, but why? Because my dear sweet wife is dead, who was the most this and the most that who ever lived! I'll never see her again; I'll never find another one like her; I've suffered an irreparable loss! O God! what have I done to Thee to merit such punishment? Why didst Thou not send death to me before her? For to live without her is but to languish. Ah, Badebec, my darling, my love, my dainty twat (it was at least five and a half acres in area), my tender little one, my codpiece, my pump, my slipper, never shall I see you again! Ah, poor Pantagruel, you have lost your good mother, your

---

[1] *in modo et figura* according to syllogistic modes and figures
[2] kite bird of the hawk family

sweet nurse, your beloved lady! Ah, false death, how evil, how outrageous thou art to have taken from me one to whom immortality rightly belonged!"

And, as he spoke, he cried like a cow. But suddenly, remembering Pantagruel, he laughed like a calf.

"Ha, my little son," he said, "my ball, my fartlet, what a fine fellow you are. How endebted I am to God who has given me such a handsome son, so gay, so happy, so fine! Ho, ho, ho, ho, how happy I am! Let's drink! Ho! let us put aside all sorrow! Bring out the best wine, rinse the glasses, set the table, drive out the dogs, poke up the fire, light the candles, close the door, slice the bread for the soup, send away these poor, give them anything they ask for. Hold my doublet. Let me put it on so as to be ready to receive the ladies."

As he said this, he heard the litany and the *Mementos*[3] of the priests who were bearing his wife off to be buried. This brought about a change in his thoughts, and suddenly he was caught up in a different kind of meditation. "Lord God," said he, "must I still be sorrowful? This bothers me. I am no longer young. I am growing old, the weather is treacherous, I might catch some fever, and then I'd be in a fine fix. Upon my faith as a gentleman, it is better to weep less and to drink more! My wife is dead; well then, by God! (*da jurandi*[4]) I'll not resurrect her with my tears. She is well off; she is in Paradise at least, if not in a better place. She is praying God for us; she is perfectly happy; she no longer has our cares, miseries, and calamities. The same fate awaits us all, and may God help the survivors! I must think about finding myself another wife.

"But here's what you can do," he said to the good midwives (Where are they? Ladies, I can't see you!), "you can go to her funeral while I stay here and rock my son, for I feel very thirsty and on the point of falling ill. Have a good drink first. You will feel all the better for it, you can take my word for it."

[3] *Mementos* prayers for the dead [4] *da jurandi* pardon my swearing

They went to the funeral as they were bid, and poor
Gargantua remained at home. He composed, however, the
following epitaph to be engraved upon Badebec's tomb-
stone:

> She died from it, my noble Badebec,
> From bearing child, whom I shall miss.
> Her face was that of a sculptured wreck,
> Her body Spanish, her Belly Swiss.[5]
> Pray God, if there be anything amiss,
> Forgive her, that she be sanctified.
> Here lies her body not too remiss,
> Which expired the year and day she died.

The Noble Pantagruel's Adolescence

Pantagruel grew and thrived visibly from day to day,
which quite naturally delighted his father. And he made
for him, when he was small, a crossbow for shooting at
little birds; and today it is known as the great crossbow of
Chantelle.[1] Eventually they sent him to school to learn and
to spend his youth.

As a matter of fact, he went to Poitiers to study, and
made great progress. Seeing that the students had so much
free time that they did not know what to do with themselves, he felt sorry for them. And so one day he took a
huge stone, twelve yards square and fourteen feet thick,
from a great rock quarry called Passelourdin,[2] and he
placed it, with no effort at all, on top of four pillars in the
middle of a field, so that the students, when they had
nothing else to do, might now spend the time climbing this
stone, having banquets on the top with many a bottle of
wine, hams and pastries, and carving their name upon it
with a knife. Today, this stone is known as the *Lifted
Stone*.[3] And, in memory of this, no student can register at

[5] the Spanish had the reputation of being slim, and the Swiss
plump   [1] **crossbow of Chantelle** huge siege engine at the castle
of Chantelle in the Bourbonnais   [2] **Passelourdin** is along the
banks of the Clain river near Poitiers   [3] ***Lifted Stone*** this dol-
men, in the region of Poitiers, is now broken

the University of Poitiers until he has drunk at the Cab-baline fountain[4] of Croutelle,[5] gone to Passelourdin, and scaled the Lifted Stone.

One day when he was reading the noble chronicles of his ancestors, Pantagruel discovered that Geoffrey de Luisignan,[6] known as Geoffrey with the Great Tooth, grandfather of the cousin-in-law of the eldest sister of the aunt of the son-in-law of the uncle of the daughter-in-law of his step-mother, was buried at Maillezais.[7] And so, like a good fellow, he took a day off to go visit him. Leaving Poitiers with a few companions, he passed through Ligugé, where he visited Ardillon, the noble abbot, through Lu-signan, Sansay, Celles, Colonges, and Fontenay-le-Comte, where he greeted the learned Tiraqueau,[8] and from there he went to Maillezais and visited the sepulchre of Geoffrey with the Great Tooth. He was somewhat frightened at his effigy, for he was depicted there as a furious warrior, with a huge broadsword half drawn. Pantagruel inquired as to the reason for this, and the canons of the place assured him that this was nothing more than *Pictoribus atque Poetis*,[9] etc., which is to say that painters and poets are entitled to paint whatever they like in any manner they choose. But he was not satisfied with this explanation, and he said:

"He has not been painted in this way without some reason. I suspect that some wrong was done him at his death, and that he expects his descendants to avenge him. I shall look further into the matter and do what seems right."

Instead of returning to Poitiers, he decided to visit the other universities of France. Proceeding to La Rochelle,

[4] **Cabbaline fountain** said to have sprung from a stroke of the foot of Pegasus, and traditionally sacred to the Muses   [5] **Crou-telle** is a village near Poitiers   [6] **Geoffrey de Luisignan** 13th century baron who lived near Poitiers   [7] **Maillezais** Benedic-tine abbey whose abbot, Geoffrey d'Estissac, was Rabelais's first patron   [8] **Ligugé . . . Tiraqueau** places and friends of Rabelais's youth   [9] Horace, *Ars poetica*, 9-10

therefore, he embarked for Bordeaux, where he found no great activity except for some longshoremen who were playing cards on the beach. From there, he went to Toulouse, where he learned how to dance very well and how to wield a two-handed sword, a tradition among the students of this university. But he did not stay there for long when he learned that they burned their professors alive as if they were red herring.[10] "God forbid that I should die that way," he exclaimed, "for I am naturally quite dry without further heating."

He went next to Montpellier, and there he found some good Mirevaux wines and joyful company. He thought of studying medicine there,[11] but he decided that this profession was too tiresome and morbid, and that physicians smelled hellishly of enemas. For this reason he thought of studying law. But, since there were only three scurvy fellows and one baldheaded legist in the place, he went on his way. In less than three hours, he made the Pont du Gard [12] and the amphitheatre at Nîmes,[13] a feat seemingly more divine than human. He then arrived at Avignon, and was not there more than three days before he fell in love, for the local ladies are great thigh-squeezers since this is papal territory.[14]

Upon perceiving this, his tutor, Epistemon[15] by name, got him out of there and took him to Valence in Dauphiné. He soon saw that very little was going on there, and that the ruffians of the town were in the habit of beating the students. This made him angry. Now one fine Sunday when everyone was dancing on the square, a student wanted to join in, and the ruffians would not let him. When Pantagruel saw this, he chased all of them to the edge of the

[10] Jean de Cahors, professor of Law, was burned alive in 1532 for heresy   [11] The tour of universities was for traditional students; Rabelais himself might have undertaken it   [12] Pont du Gard Roman aqueduct near Arles   [13] amphitheatre at Nîmes also of Roman construction   [14] Avignon was Papal territory until the French Revolution; it was famous for its women of easy virtue   [15] Epistemon name meaning the Learned

Rhone, and he would have drowned them if they had not burrowed into the earth like moles a good two miles under the river. The hole may still be seen there today.[16]

After this he went on his way, and arrived in Angers in three hops and a jump. He liked it very much and would have stayed but for the plague. Next he came to Bourges, where he studied a long time, and learned a great deal at the College of Law. He said at times that law books were like a fine gold robe, marvelously brilliant and precious, but bordered with excrement. "For," he said, "no books on earth are so beautiful, so decorated, so elegant as the text of the *Pandects*,[17] but their borders—that is to say the glosses of Accursius[18]—are so soiled, foul, and polluted that they are nothing but filth and rot."

Leaving Bourges, he went to Orléans, and there he found many a swaggering scholar to celebrate his arrival. In no time at all he learned from them how to play tennis so well that he became a master of it, for the students there were much given to the game. They took him to the islands[19] sometimes to play push-in. For fear of straining his eyes, Pantagruel made sure not to study too hard— especially since one of the professors repeated frequently in his lectures that nothing is more harmful to the sight than a malady of the eyes. Now one day when the degree of Master of Law was conferred upon one of the students he knew—one who had about as much learning as you could put in your hand, but who was an expert at dancing and playing tennis—Pantagruel wrote the following blazon[20] in honor of the graduates of the University:

> A tennis ball in pocket and
> A racket in your busy hand,
> A law book in your student hood,
> And feet that learned to dance but good,
> Doctor of Law, at last, you stand.

[16] a subterranean passage existed under the Rhone at this place until the 17th century [17] *Pandects* digest of Roman civil law [18] **Accursius** famous medieval commentator of Roman law [19] islands in the Loire [20] **blazon** coat of arms

How Pantagruel Met a Limousin who Deformed the French Language

One day, I cannot say when, Pantagruel was walking with his friends after dinner near the gate which one takes for Paris. He met a student here, as natty as could be, coming down the road. After they had greeted one another, Pantagruel inquired: "Where are you coming from, my friend, at this time of day?"

The student replied: "From the alme, inclyte and celebrate academy which is vocitated Lutetia." [1]

"What is he saying?" Pantagruel asked one of his men.

"He means," came the reply, "from Paris."

"So you're coming from Paris, are you?" Pantagruel continued. "And how do you young gentlemen students spend your time in Paris?"

The scholar answered: "We transfretate the Sequana at the dilucule and crespuscule; we deambulate through the compites and quadrivies of the urbe; we despumate the Latin verbocination and, like verisimile armorabonds, we captate the benevolence of the omnijugal, omniform, and omnigenous muliebrine sex. Certain diecules we invisitate the lupanars, and in veneric ecstasy we inculcate our virilia into the penetissim recesses of the pudends of those supremely amicable meretricules. Then we proceed to pabulate in the mercantile taverns of the Pine Apple, the Castle, the Magdalen, and the Mule, rare vervecine spatules, perforaminated with petrosil. If by misfortune there be rarity or penury of pecune in our marusupies, or if they be exhausted of ferruginus metal, we demit our codices and oppignerate our vestments to pay while prestolating the arrival of tabellaries from our patriotic lares and penates." [2]

[1] **From . . . Lutetia** From the cherishing, illustrious and celebrated University of Paris [2] **We . . . penates** We cross the Seine at dawn and at dusk; we stroll through the squares and streets of the city; we mouth the Latin language, and like true lovers, we obtain the kindness of the feminine sex which decides all, assumes all forms, and engenders all. At

"What the devil kind of language is this?" cried Pantagruel. "By God, you must be a heretic of some kind."

"Signor, no," replied the student, "for libentissimally, as soon as there illuscesces any minutule fragment of day, I demigrate into one of those well-architected ecclesiastical abodes, and there, irrorating myself with fine lustral water, I nibble a piece of missic precation of our sacrificules. Submurmurating my horarian precules, I elave and absterge my anima of its nocturnal inquinations. I revere the Olympicoles, I venere latrially the supernal Astripotent, I dilige and redame my proxims. I observe the decalogical precepts, and, according to the facultatule of my vires, I do not discede from them one unguicule. It is quite veriform that since Mammon does not supergurgitate anything in my loculs, I am somewhat rare and tardigrade in supererogating the eleemosyn to these indigents who hostially queritate their stipend." [3]

"Turd, a turd!" said Pantagruel. "What does this fool

certain times we visit the houses of prostitution, and in the ecstasy inspired by Venus, we insert our viril members into the very deep recesses of the secret parts of these very friendly little whores; then at the taverns known as the Pine Apple, the Castle, the Madeleine, and the Mule, we eat fine shoulders of mutton larded with parsley. And if, by chance, there is a rarity or penury of money in our pocketbooks, and if they be empty of iron coins, we pawn our books and clothing while waiting for the arrival of messengers from home   [3] **Signor . . . stipend** "Sir, no," replied the student, "for very willingly as soon as shines the slightest light of dawn, I go into one of those well-built churches, and there, sprinkling myself with holy water, I take in the mass prayers of the priests. Mumbling my prayers according to canonical hours, I wash and clean my soul of its nocturnal stains. I worship the heavenly powers, I venerate with devotion the supreme sovereign of the stars, I love my neighbors and return their love. I keep the precepts of the Decalogue, and, to the limit of my poor strength, I do not stray from them in the slightest. It is quite true that since Mammon [god of wealth] does not spit up a thing into my pocketbook, I am a bit slow in giving alms to these poor people who beg money from door to door" mean? I think he's forging some kind of diabolic tongue as he goes along, and that he's trying to bewitch us all, like an enchanter."

One of his friends then spoke up: "No doubt this rascal is attempting to imitate the language of the Parisians; but all he is doing is flaying Latin and he thinks he's Pindarizing. It probably seems to him that he's quite an orator in French because he doesn't talk like everyone else."

"Is this true?" Pantagruel asked.

The student replied: "Ah, signor, my genius is not natively adept to what this flagitious nebulon manifests, that is, excoriating the cuticule of your Gallic vernacular; but I applicate my scruples viceversally and then with the auxiliary of veles and rames enite to locupletate it with a Latinicome redundancy." [4]

"By God," said Pantagruel, "I'll teach you how to talk. But first, tell me where you're from."

"The primeval origin of my aves and ataves," replied the student, "was indigenous to the Lemovican regions where requiesces the corpor of the hagiotate St. Martial." [5]

"I understand now," said Pantagruel. "You're a Limousin to the teeth, and you're trying to imitate a Parisian. Come here, and I'll give you a dressing down!"

Then he took the student by the throat and said to him: "You flay Latin, do you? By St. John, I'll make you flay the fox,[6] for I'm going to flay you alive!"

Then the poor Limousin began to sputter: "Hey, squire! Ho, St. Martial! Help! Ahhhh! Let me go, for God's sake! Don't touch me!"

And Pantagruel said: "Now you're talking naturally."

[4] **Ah . . . redundancy** "My lord, I have no intention of doing what this infamous rascal speaks of, that is, skinning the French language, but, on the contrary, I work zealously and go full sail in an attempt to enrich it with a Latin-like redundancy"
[5] **The . . . Martial** "My forefathers and ancestors come from the Limousin where lies the body of the very holy St. Martial"
[6] **flay the fox** to vomit

And he let him go, for the poor devil had completely be-
fouled his breeches, which were cut in the back in codfish-
tail fashion, and not with a full bottom.

"By St. Alipentin," [7] exclaimed Pantagruel, "what a
mess! The devil take this turnip-eater,[8] he stinks so!"

And he let him go. But the student felt remorse for this
all his life, and was always so thirsty that he would often
say that Pantagruel had him by the throat. A few years
later he died the death of Roland,[9] fulfilling thereby divine
vengeance, and demonstrating what the philosopher and
Aulus Gellius have said,[10] that it is better to speak simply,
and, as Octavius Augustus once said,[11] we should steer
clear of unusual words even as masters of ships avoid reefs
at sea.

How Pantagruel, while in Paris, Received a Letter from his Father and the Copy Thereof

Pantagruel studied very hard, as you might well imagine,
and profited greatly thereby; for he had a double supply
of intelligence, and the capacity of his memory was as
great as twelve casks of olives. While studying there, he
received one day the following letter from his father:

My dear son,

Among the gifts, graces, and prerogatives with which
the sovereign Creator, God Almighty, has endowed and
embellished human nature from its beginning, the one
which seems to me most singular and excellent is the one
which enables us to acquire a kind of immortality and, in
the course of this transitory life, perpetuate our name and
seed. This is accomplished by progeny born of us in lawful
wedlock. Thus is restored to us in a measure what was lost
through the sin of our first parents, who were told that,

---

[7] **St. Alipentin** is a facetious saint   [8] **turnip-eater** name given the
Limousins   [9] **death of Roland** a death due to thirst, according
to popular tradition   [10] **philosopher and Aulus Gellius** the philosopher Favorinus said this according to *The Attic Nights* of
Aulus Gellius   [11] once again, according to Aulus Gellius

because they had disobeyed the commandment of God the Creator, they would die and, by death, the magnificent form in which man was created would be reduced to nothingness. But, by means of seminal propagation, there remains in children what was lost in the parents, and in grandchildren what perished in children, and so on, from generation to generation, until the hour of the Last Judgment when Jesus Christ shall restore to God the Father His Kingdom, pacified, secured, and cleansed of sin. Then will cease all generation and corruption, and the elements will no longer continue transmutations, in view of the fact that peace so anxiously desired shall have been attained and perfected, and all things shall have been brought to their end and period.

Not without just and equitable cause do I give thanks, therefore, to God my Saviour, for having granted me the gift of beholding my old age blossom anew in your youth, for, when, by His pleasure, who rules and orders all, my soul shall leave this human habitation, I shall not consider myself to be dying completely, but, rather, to be passing from one place to another, since in you and by you, my visible image remains on earth, living, seeing, and conversing with men of honor and with my friends as I myself was wont. My conduct has not been, I confess, without sin (for we all transgress and must continually ask God to erase our sins), but it has been without reproach.

This is why, since my corporal image resides in you, if my spiritual qualities did not also shine there, then you would not be considered the guardian and treasurer of the immortality of our name, and the pleasure I should derive, this being the case, would be small, considering that the least part of me, which is the body, would remain, and the best, which is the soul, through which our name remains blessed among men, would be degenerated and bastardized. I say this not out of doubt of your virtue, which has already been proved to me, but to encourage you more strongly to constant improvement. And what I am writing you now is not so much to confirm you in the virtuous course you are living as to make you rejoice at the fact that you are living and have lived in this way, and to give you added strength for the future.

To help you carry out and complete this enterprize, it is sufficient for you to remember that I have spared nothing, but have helped you as though I had no other treasure in this world than the joy of seeing you, once in my life, absolutely perfect in virtue, honesty, and valor, as well as in all liberal and worthy knowledge, and of leaving you after my death as a mirror reflecting your father's image and, if not altogether as excellent or as perfect as I might wish you to be, at least with a desire on your part to become so.

While my late father of blessed memory, Grandgousier, devoted all his efforts to seeing that I might profit from every perfection and political wisdom, and while my labors and studies were equal to his desires and even surpassed them, nevertheless, as you can readily understand, the times were not as suitable nor favorable to learning as they are today, nor did I ever have the abundance of gifted teachers which you have. We were still in the dark ages, suffering from the unfortunate calamity brought about by the destruction of all good literature by the Goths.[1] But, by divine goodness, light and dignity have been brought back to letters during my lifetime, and I now see such improvement that I should find it difficult to enter the bottom class of a grammar school, I who, in the prime of life, was reputed (not erroneously) the most learned man of the century. I tell you this not in a spirit of vain boasting, although I might justifiably do so in writing to you, on the authority of Marcus Tullius[2] in his book *Of Old Age,* and of Plutarch in his *How a Man May Praise Himself Without Envy,* but merely to give you a desire to aim ever higher.

Now all the branches of science have been reestablished and languages have been restored: Greek, without which a man would be ashamed to be called learned, Hebrew,

[1] **Goths** barbarians in general   [2] **Marcus Tullius** Cicero

Chaldean, and Latin. Printing, so elegant and exact an art, invented during my lifetime through divine inspiration, just as, on the other hand, artillery was invented at the suggestion of the devil. The world is full of learned men, erudite teachers, vast libraries, and I do not believe that the age of Plato, Cicero, or Papinian[3] afforded such facilities for study as now exist. It is now unthinkable for anyone to appear either in a public place or in private company who has not been sufficiently polished in Minerva's[4] workshop. I see robbers, hangmen, adventurers, and jockeys of today who are more learned than the doctors and preachers of my time. Why, even women and girls aspire to the glory and heavenly manna of learning. Thus, at my advanced age, I have been obliged to take up Greek. Not that I had despised it like Cato; I just did not have the chance to learn it in my youth. And I now derive great pleasure from reading Plutarch's *Morals,* the noble *Dialogues* of Plato, the *Monuments* of Pausanias, and the *Antiquities* of Athenaeus as I await the hour when it shall please God, my Creator, to call and command me to leave this earth.

This is why, my son, I admonish you to use your youth making the most of your studies and virtues. You are in Paris, you have your tutor Epistemon; the one can inspire you by direct oral teaching, the other by noble example.

I intend and insist that you learn languages perfectly. First, Greek, as Quintilian suggests; secondly, Latin, and then Hebrew for Holy Scriptures, as well as Chaldean and Arabic. Model your Greek style on Plato, your Latin style on Cicero. Let there be no detail of history with which you are not familiar. In this you will find the various works which have been written on cosmography to be of great help.

As for the liberal arts, geometry, arithmetic, and music, I gave you a taste of them where you were only a lad of five or six. Keep them up, and learn all the rules of astron-

[3] **Papinian** (3rd century A.D.) Roman jurist of enormous erudition [4] **Minerva** goddess of wisdom

omy. Have nothing to do with astrology and the divinatory art of Lullius,[3] for these are but vanity and imposture. As for civil law, I want you to know the best texts by heart, and to be able to compare them to philosophy.

A knowledge of nature is indispensable, and I would have you apply yourself to it so that there be no sea, river, stream of which you do not know the fish. Be familiar as well with all the birds of the air, all the trees, bushes, shrubs of the forests, all the herbs, all the metals hidden in the bowels of the earth, the precious stones in the orient and the south.

Then read carefully the books of the Greek, Arab, and Latin physicians, without slighting the Talmudists and Cabbalists,[4] and, by frequent dissections, acquire a perfect knowledge of that other world which is man. And devote a few hours of the day to the study of Holy Writ; first the New Testament and the Epistles of the Apostles in Greek, then the Old Testament in Hebrew. In short, become an abysm of knowledge, for now that you are becoming a grown man, you will soon have to give up your studious retreat so as to learn chivalry and the bearing of arms, in order to be able to defend my house and protect our allies in all their affairs against the attack of evildoers. And I want you to see how much you have profited from your studies. This you can do in no better way than by public discussions and debate on any subject against all comers, and by frequenting learned men in Paris and elsewhere.

But since, as Solomon the wise said, wisdom does not enter into a malicious soul and science without conscience is but the ruin of the soul, you should serve, love, and fear God, and place in Him all your thoughts and hopes. With a faith formed through charity, cling to Him in such a way that sin may never come between you. Hold suspect the abuses of the world; set not your heart upon vanity, for

[3] allusion to the *Ars brevis* of Raymond Lully, alchemist and philosopher of the latter half of the 13th century   [4] **Talmudists and Cabbalists** commentators of Jewish civil and religious laws as well as of Scriptures

this life is transitory, but the word of God lives eternally. Be of service to all your neighbors, and love them as yourself. Honor your teachers, flee the company of people you do not wish to resemble, and receive not in vain the graces that God has given you. When you feel that you have acquired all the knowledge that you can in Paris, come back to me so that I may give you my blessing before I die.

My son, may the peace and grace of our Lord be with you. Amen.

From Utopia, the seventeenth day of March.
Your father,

Gargantua.

How Pantagruel Found Panurge, whom he Loved all his Life

One day, as he was walking outside the city near St. Anthony's Abbey,[1] conversing and philosophizing with his followers and a few students, Pantagruel came upon a man, handsome in stature and body, but grievously wounded in several places and in such bad condition generally that he looked as though he had escaped from the dogs, or, rather, like a Norman scarecrow. As soon as Pantagruel caught sight of him, he said to those who were with him: "Do you see this man coming along the Charenton Bridge road?[2] Take my word for it, he is poor in fortune only. I can tell from his physiognomy that Nature produced him from a rich and noble family, but that the misadventures which beset the curious have reduced him to this penury and poverty."

And as soon as the stranger reached them, Pantagruel said to him: "My friend, would you be so kind as to stop and answer a few questions. You won't regret it, for I should like very much to help you. I can see that you are in trouble, and I am very sorry for you. Tell me, friend,

[1] **St. Anthony's Abbey** Cistercian abbey, demolished in **1796**, which stood not far from the Place de la Bastille in Paris
[2] **Charenton Bridge road** ran from what is now the Place de la Bastille to the suburb of Charenton

who are you? Where do you come from? Where are you going? What are you looking for? And what is your name?"

The stranger answered him as follows:

"Junker, Gott geb euch Glück unnd Hail. Zuvor, lieber Juncker, ich las euch wissen, das da ihr mich von fragt, ist ein arm unnd erbarmglich Ding, unnd wer vil darvon zu sagen, welches euch verdruslich zu hoeren, unnd mir zu erzelen wer, vievol, die Poeten unnd Orators vorzeiten haben gesagt in iren Sprüchen und Sententzen, das die Gedechtnus des Ellends unnd Armuot vorlangst erlitten ist ain grosser Lust." [3]

To which Pantagruel replied: "My friend, I do not understand this gibberish. If you want me to understand, you'll have to speak some other language."

The stranger replied:

"Al barildim gotfano dech min brin alabo dordin falbroth ringuam albaras. Nin porth zadilkin almucathim milko prim al elmin enthoth dal heben ensouim: kuth im al dim alkatim nim broth dechoth porth min michas im endoth, pruch dal maisoulum hol moth dansririm lupaldas im voldemoth. Nin hur diavolth mnarbothim del gousch pal frapin duch im scoth pruch galeth dal chinon, min foulthrich al conin butathen doth dal prim." [4]

"Can you figure that out?" Pantagruel asked the others.

"I think it is the language of the Antipodes," said Epistemon. "Not even the devil could figure it out."

"My friend," Pantagruel said, "I don't know whether the walls understand you, but none of us does, not a single syllable."

The stranger then said:

---

[3] [German] "My lord, may God give you happiness and prosperity. In the first place, my dear lord, I must advise you that what you ask of me pains me deeply and would make a story tiresome for you to listen to and for me to tell, even though poets and orators of old, in their adages and sentences, do say that remembering past hardships and sufferings is a great joy"
[4] gibberish of Rabelais's invention in which one discerns certain proper names (Frapin, Chinon)

"Signor mio, voi vedete per essempio cha la cornamuse non suona mai s'ela non a il ventre pieno; cosi io parimente non vi saprei contare le mie fortune, se prima il tribulato ventre non a la solita refectione, al quale è adviso che le mani et le denti habbiano perso il loro ordine naturale et del tuto annichillati." [5]

"We're no better off than before," said Epistemon.

The stranger then went on:

"Lard, ghest tholb be sua virtiuss be intelligence ass yi body schall biss be naturall relvtht, tholb suld of me pety have, for nature hass ulss egually maide; bot fortune sum exaltit hess, an oyis deprevit. Non ye less viois mou virtius deprevit and virtiuss men discrivis, for, anen ye lad end, iss non gud." [6]

"I still don't get you," said Pantagruel.

Then the stranger said:

"Jona andie, guaussa goussyetan behar da er remedio beharde versela ysser landa. Anbates oyto y es nausu eyn essassu gour ray proposian ordine den. Nonyssena bayta facheria egabeb genherassy badia sadassu nouraa ssia. Aran Hondouan gualde cydassu nay dassuna. Estou oussyc eguinan soury hin er darstura eguy harm. Genicoa plasar vadu." [7]

"Are you Genicoa then?" [8] asked Eudemon.

[5] [Italian] "My lord, you can see, for example, that the bagpipe never plays unless it has a full belly. It's the same thing with me—I cannot tell you of my adventures if my troubled belly does not first have its customary refreshment. It is of the opinion that my hands and teeth have forgotten how to work and are completely annihilated" [6] [Scotch English] "My lord, if you are as powerful in intelligence as you are naturally big in body, you should have pity on me: for nature made us equal, but fortune has exalted some and debased others. Nevertheless, virtue is often disdained and virtuous men despised, for before the final end no one is good" [7] [In Basque] "My lord for all ills there must be a remedy; to do what is right, this is difficult. I have begged you so! Let there be some sort of system in our proposals; that will occur, without any difficulty, if you have me brought something to eat. After that, ask me what you will. It wouldn't be a bad thing for you to pay for both of us, God willing" [8] **Genicoa** from God

"By St. Trinian, you're from Scotland!" said Carpalim,[9] "or I didn't understand you."

The stranger continued:

"Prug frest frins sorgdmand strochdt drhds pag brlelang Gravot Chavigny Pomardière rusth pkalhdracg Devinière près Nays. Bouille kalmuch monach drupp delmeupplist rincq dlrndodelb up drent loch minc stz rinquald de vins ders cordelis but jocststzampenards." [10]

"Are you talking Christian, my friend," asked Epistemon, "or Patelinese?" [11]

"No, that's Lanternese," [12] someone interjected.

But the stranger went on:

"Heere, ie en spreeke anders geen taele, dan kersten taele: my dunct nochtans, al en seg ie u niet een woordt mynen nood verklaart ghenonch wat ie beglere; gheest my wyt bermherticheyt yet waer un ie ghevoed magh zunch." [13]

"I understand as much of that," said Pantagruel, "as I did of the other."

"Seignor, de tanto hablar yo soy cansado. Por que suplico a Vuestra Reverencia que mire a los preceptos evangelicos, para que ellos movant Vuertra Reverencia a lo que es de consciencia; y si ellos non bastarent para mover Vuestra Reverencia a piedad, yo supplico que mire a la piedad natural, la qual yo creo que le movra como es de razon, y con esto non digo mas." [14]

[9] **Carpalim** Pantagruel's messenger His name means Rapid [10] Language of Rabelais's invention. We recognize Gravot, Clavigny, Pomardière, Devinière, which were lands belonging to the Rabelais family [11] **Patelinese** gibberish spoken by Patelin in the 15th century farce of the same name [12] **Lanternese** imaginary language [13] [Dutch] "My lord, I do not speak any language that is not Christian; it seems to me nevertheless that, even if I don't say a word, my rags ought to tell you what I want. Be charitable enough to give me a bit of refreshment" [14] [Spanish] "Lord, I am tired of so much talking. And so I beg Your Reverence to consider the Gospel precepts, so that they may direct Your Reverence to do what conscience requires, and if they do not suffice in inciting Your Reverence to pity, I beg him to consider natural pity which, I believe, will sway him; with these words, I say no more"

"Indeed, my friend," said Pantagruel, "I've no doubt that you can speak several languages very well; but tell me what you want in some language we can understand."

"Myn Herre, endog, jeg med inghen tunge ta lede, lygeson boeen, ocg uskuulig creatner! Myne Kleebon och my ne legoms magerhed udviser alligue kladig huuad tyng meg meest behoff girered somder sandeligh mad och drycke: hvuarpor forbarme teg omsyder offuermeg; oc befarlat gyffuc meg nogueth; aff hvylket ieg kand styre myne groeendes magher lygeruff son man Cerbero en soppe forsetthr. Soa shal tuloeffue lenge och lycksaligth." [15]

"I think," Eustenes[16] said, "that is how the Goths speak. And, were God willing, we would all speak through our hindends like this!"

Then the stranger said:

"Adoni, scholom lecha: im ischar harob hal habdeca, bemeherah thithen il kikar lehem, chancatbub: Laah al Adonia chonenral." [17]

"Ha!" cried Epistemon, "this time I understand. That's Hebrew, most grammatically spoken."

But the stranger went on:

"Despota tinyn panagathe, diati sy mi uc artodotis? Horas gar limo analiscomenon eme athlios. Ce en to metaxy eme uc eleis udamos, zetis de par emu ha u chre, ce homos philologi pantes homologusi tote logus te kerhemata peritta hyparchin, opote pragma afto pasi delon esti. Entha gar anankei monon logi isin, hina pragmata (hon peri amphisbetumen) me phosphoros epiphenete." [18]

"Why!" said Carpalim, Pantagruel's lackey, "that's Greek!

---

[15] [Danish] "Sir, even in the event that, like children and animals, I should not speak any language, my clothing and the emaciation of my body would show what I stand in need of, which is, to eat and drink. Have pity on me, therefore, and have me given something to muzzle the barkings of my stomach, just as one puts soup in front of Cerberus. Thus shall you live long and happy"   [16] Eustenes name meaning Powerful   [17] [Hebrew] "Sir, peace be with you. If you wish to do good to your servant, give me a loaf of bread, as it is written: He lends to the Lord who has pity on the poor"   [18] [Greek] "Excellent master, why don't you give me bread? You see me perishing miser-

I understand that. How is it that you know it? Have you lived in Greece?"

The stranger answered:

"Agonou dont oussys vou denaguez algarou, nou den farou zamist vou mariston ulbrou, fousquez vou brol tam bredaguezmoupreton den goul houst, daguez daguez nou croupys fost bardou noflist nou grou. Agou paston tol nalprissys hourtou los echatonous, prou dhouguys brol panygou den bascrou nou dous cagnous goulfren goul oust troppassou." [19]

"I think I understand that," said Pantagruel, "for that's either the language of my country of Utopia, or else it's very much like it in sound."

But as he was about to address him, the stranger went on:

"Jam toties vos, per sacra, perque deos deaque omnis obtestatus sum, ut, si qua vos pietas permovet, egestatem meam solaremini, nec hilum proficio clamans et ejulans. Sinite, queso, sinite, viri impii. *Quo me fata vocant* abire, nec ultra vanis vestris interpellationibus obtundatis, memores veteris illius adagii, quo venter famelicus auriculis carere dicitur." [20]

"By God, my friend," cried Pantagruel, "can't you speak French?"

"Of course, very well, my lord," said the stranger. "It's my native and maternal language, praise God, for I was born and brought up in Touraine, the garden of France."

"Then tell us," said Pantagruel, "what your name is and

ably of hunger, and yet you have no pity on me and ask me questions out of season. But all lovers of letters realize that speech and words are superfluous when the facts speak for themselves. Words are necessary only when the facts under discussion don't show it clearly"   [19] Language of Rabelais's invention.   [20] [Latin] "Several times already, by all that is sacred, by all the gods and goddesses, I have begged you, if you can be moved by pity, to relieve my distress, but I'm getting nowhere with my cries and complaints. Permit me, I beg you, permit me, impious me, to go where fate calls me, and do not tire me further with your vain questions, remembering this old adage which says that a hungry belly has no ears" where you come from; for, I swear, I have already taken such a fancy to you that if you wish, you need never stir from my side, and you and I will be friends as Aeneas and Achates were."

"My lord," was the reply, "my true and proper Christian name is Panurge, and I am just on my way back from Turkey where I was taken prisoner on the ill-fated expedition to Mytilene.[21] I'd be delighted to tell you of my adventures, for they are more marvelous than those of Ulysses; but since you have invited me to remain with you (and I accept the invitation most gladly, promising never to leave you, even if you go to all the devils), we shall have lots of time for all that a bit later. Just now I feel a most urgent impulse to eat. My teeth are on edge, my belly is empty, my throat is dry, my appetite is crying out, everything is all set. If you want to put me to work, it will be a sight for sore eyes to watch me eat. For God's sake, see to it!"

Pantagruel then instructed that he be taken to his lodgings, and brought lots of food. This was done, and Panurge ate very well that evening. He went to bed with the chickens and slept until dinner time the next day. He had only to take three hops and a jump, therefore, in order to get from his bed to the table.

HOW PANTAGRUEL COVERED A WHOLE ARMY WITH HIS TONGUE AND WHAT THE AUTHOR SAW IN HIS MOUTH

When Pantagruel, with all his followers, entered the land of the Dipsodes,[1] everybody was overjoyed and surrendered to him immediately. They delivered to him of their own free will the keys of all their cities—all except the Almyrodes[2] who wanted to resist and who replied to his heralds that they would surrender only under certain conditions.

[21] The French besieged this Greek island in 1502, but were repulsed by the Turks   [1] **Dipsodes** the Thirsty Ones   [2] **Almyrodes** the Briny Ones

"What better conditions could they ask for than a hand on the jug and a glass in the fist?" asked Pantagruel. "Come on, let's go sack them." At once, they all fell into rank, ready to attack.

But on the way, as they were going through a vast stretch of open country, they were caught in a heavy rain. At this, they began to shiver and to crowd together. Seeing what was happening, Pantagruel had the captains tell them that it was nothing serious, that he could see over the clouds, and that it would be nothing more than a little mist; nevertheless, let them keep ranks, and he would shelter them. The men put themselves in close order, and Pantagruel extended his tongue only half way, and covered them with it as a hen covers her chicks.

Meanwhile I, who am telling you these most truthful tales, had hidden myself under a burdock leaf almost as large as the arch of the Mantrible bridge;[3] but when I saw Pantagruel's men so well sheltered, I decided to take shelter with them. But there were so many of them that I was unable to, for, as the saying goes, "there's no cloth left at the end of the roll." As best I could, therefore, I climbed up and travelled a good two leagues along his tongue before entering his mouth.

But, O gods and goddesses, what did I see there? May Jupiter confound me with his three-pronged lightning if I'm lying. I was able to stroll around in there as one does in St. Sophia's at Constantinople. And I saw rocks as big as the mountains of Denmark (I believe they were his teeth), and vast meadows, great forests, and large and strong cities, no less populous than Lyons or Poitiers.

The first person I encountered was a chap planting cabbages. I asked of him in astonishment:

"What are you doing here, my friend?"

"Planting cabbages," he replied.

"Why? How?"

"Ha, sir, we can't all have balls as heavy as a mortar,

[3] **Mantrible bridge** figures in *Fierabras*, a popular chivalric novel of the day

and we can't all be rich. This is the way I earn a living, and I take and sell them in the city over yonder."

"Good Lord! Is this a new world?"

"There's absolutely nothing new about it. But they say that there is a new land outside where there is a sun and a moon, and all kinds of fine things; but this one is much older."

"Well, my friend, but what is the name of the town where you sell your cabbages?"

"It's called Aspharage.[4] Its citizens are good Christians, honest, and will treat you most kindly."

On his recommendation, I decided to go there.

Now, on my way, I came upon a man who was trapping pigeons, and I asked him:

"Friend, where do your pigeons come from?"

"Sir," he said, "they come from the other world."

I concluded that the pigeons must enter Pantagruel's mouth in flocks when he yawned, thinking it a dovecot.

I soon entered the city which I found handsome, strong, and pleasantly situated. The sentries at the gate, however, asked me for a health certificate. I was very surprised at this, and I asked them:

"Gentlemen, is there danger of the plague here?"

"My lord," they said, they've been dying all over the place, as fast as the cart can travel through the streets."

"Good God!" I said, "and where?"

They told me that the plague was raging in Larynx and Pharynx, two cities as large as Rouen and Nantes, rich and bustling. And the cause of the plague was a stinking, noxious exhalation which had been coming from the abyss for some time now. And more then twenty-two hundred and seventy-six thousand and sixteen people had died from it in the past eight days. I stopped then to do a little meditating, and finally realized that this exhalation must be an unsavory breath emanating from Pantagruel's stomach, from his having eaten too much garlic stew.

[4] **Aspharage** City of the Throat

Going on from there, I passed among the rocks which were his teeth, and even climbed one of them and found the most beautiful spot in the world, with fine large tennis courts, spacious galleries, lovely meadows, plentiful vines, and an infinity of country houses built in the Italian style in the midst of delightful fields. I spent a good four months here and never had a better time in my life.

Then I climbed down by the back teeth towards the lips, but I was robbed by brigands on the way, in a huge forest near the ears. Then I found a little village on a slope (I've forgotten its name) where I had even a better time than before. I even earned some money to live on. Do you know how? By sleeping! For they rent people to sleep by the day, and it's possible to make five or six pennies a day at it. Those who snore loudly enough earn seven and a half pennies. I told the senators that I had been robbed in the valley, and they said that the people over there were a villainous lot, and just naturally brigands. From this I realized that just as we have countries on the near and far side of the mountains, they have them on the near and far side of the teeth. But it is much better living on this side, and the climate is healthier.

I then began to think how true the statement is that half the world doesn't know how the other half lives. No one had yet written about this country, and yet there are in it more than twenty-five inhabited kingdoms, not counting the deserts and vast stretches of sea. But I have now composed a voluminous book on the subject, called the *History of the Gorgians*[5]—this is what I have called them since they live in the throat of my master Pantagruel.

Finally, I was ready to return, and going down his beard, I landed on his shoulders, and from there I slid to the ground and fell right in front of him. When he saw me, he asked:

"Where have you been, Alcofribas?" [6]

"In your throat, sir."

[5] **Gorgians** Inhabitants of the Throat   [6] **Alcofribas** Rabelais himself!

"How long have you been there?"

"Since you went to war with the Almyrodes."

"That was more than six months ago. And how did you live, what did you drink?"

"The same as you, my lord. I had my share of the tastiest bits you put between your lips."

"Indeed," he said, "but where did you defecate?"

"In your throat," I said.

"Ha, ha, what a good fellow you are," he said. "Since you left, we have conquered, with God's help, all of Dipsody. I hereby make you a present of the domain of Salmagundi." [7]

"Many thanks, my lord. You reward me beyond what I deserve," I said.

THE CONCLUSION OF THIS BOOK AND THE AUTROR'S APOLOGY

Now gentlemen, you have heard the beginning of the horrendous story of my Lord and Master Pantagruel. I will terminate my first book here because my head aches a bit, and I think that the registers of my brain have been somewhat blurred by this septembral vintage.[1]

You will have the rest of the story at the next Frankfort fair.[2] Then you will see how Panurge was married and cuckolded the very first month of his marriage; how Pantagruel found the philosopher's stone, and the way to find one and make use of it; how he crossed the Caspian Mountains; how he sailed the Atlantic Ocean, vanquished the cannibals, and conquered the Pearl Islands;[3] how he married the daughter of Prester John,[4] King of India; how he fought against the devils and burned five chambers of Hell, put to sack the great black chamber and threw Persephone[5] into the fire, broke four of Lucifer's teeth

[7] **Salmagundi** is a kind of stew   [1] **septembral vintage** new wine
[2] **Frankfort fair** Germany; one of the most famous fairs of the time, held twice a year   [3] **Pearl Islands** in the Antilles   [4] **Prester John** legendary person   [5] **Persephone** daughter of Zeus and Demeter, abducted to the underworld by Pluto

and the horn on his rump; how he visited the regions of the moon to find out if, in fact, the moon is whole or if women have three-quarters of it in their heads; and a thousand other jolly little anecdotes, all of them true. It's fine stuff, I assure you.

Good night, gentlemen. *Perdonate mi,*[6] as the Italians say, and do not think so much of my faults that you forget your own.

If you should say to me: "Sir, it would seem that you were not very wise to write all this twaddle and pleasant nonsense," my answer to you would be that you are hardly any wiser to be spending your time reading it. But if you read it as a pleasant pastime, just as I have written it to pass the time, then you are more worthy of pardon than a great lot of dissolute monks, moral lepers, snails, hypocrites, bedbugs, humbugs, and other bugs, who have got themselves all rigged up in masks to deceive the world. For, giving the public to understand that they spend all their time in contemplation and devotion, in fastings and macerations of their sensual nature, that their only concern is to sustain and nourish the fragile spark of human nature that is in them, what they really are doing is having a good time, and God knows how! *Et Curios simulant, sed bacchanalia vivunt.*[7] You can read it in big illuminated letters on their red snouts and pot-bellies, unless they should perfume themselves with sulphur.[8]

As for their studies, they read only Pantagrueline books. But not so much to pass the time cheerfully as to harm someone viciously, namely, by beassing, fartassing, and twistassing, by buttocking, ballocking, and devilsocking, that is, by calumniating. In so doing, they are like village clods who, in cherry season, make a business out of digging into and stirring around the excrement of little children

---

[6] *Perdonate mi* Excuse me, in Italian   [7] *Et . . . vivunt* They imitate the Curii, but live like Bacchanals. The Curii were known for the sobriety; the Bacchanals for their riotous living   [8] in order to appear pale

in search of stones which they then sell to druggists for Mahaleb oil.[9]

Flee, abhor, and hate all these as much as I do, and you will be all the better for it, I assure you. And if you wish to be good Pantagruelists, that is, to live in peace, joy, health, enjoying yourselves always, then never put your faith in people who look through a peephole.[10]

[9] **Mahaleb oil** was used in making perfume   [10] such as monks, through their hoods

THE THIRD BOOK

Of the Heroic Deeds and Sayings
of the Worthy Pantagruel

COMPOSED BY M. FRANÇOIS RABELAIS
DOCTOR OF MEDICINE

How Panurge Got a Bug in his Ear and Stopped Wearing his Magnificent Codpiece

Panurge had his right ear pierced in the Jewish fashion, and a little gold ring of damascene workmanship attached to it. A flea was enchased in the setting. And the flea was black, so you need not bother yourself about that any more (it is a marvelous thing to be well informed), and its upkeep, as reported by his office, barely amounted to more per quarter than the marriage of a Hyracanian[1] tigress, that is to say some 600,000 maravedis.[2] When he was done paying for it, he was annoyed at his extravagance; thereafter, like any tyrant or lawyer, he proceeded to take it out of the sweat and blood of his subjects.

He then took four ells of coarse brown cloth, draped it about him like a long closed coat, stopped wearing his breeches, and attached a pair of spectacles to his bonnet. He appeared before Pantagruel dressed in this way. Pantagruel found the disguise strange, especially since he no longer saw the handsome and magnificent codpiece which used to constitute Panurge's last refuge against all the storms of adversity. Unable to fathom this mystery, the good Pantagruel inquired as to the significance of this new prosopopoeia.

[1]**Hyracania** part of ancient Persia   [2]**maravedis** Spanish coins

"I have a flea in my ear," replied Panurge. "I want to get married."

"That's fine," said Pantagruel, "I'm delighted to hear this. But I shouldn't want to have to swear that you'll go through with it. Lovers don't usually go around with their breeches off, their shirts hanging down about their knees, wearing a long robe of coarse brown cloth—an unusual color for men of worth and quality. If a few heretics and sectarians have worn it in the past (even though many attributed it to trickery, imposture, and desire to mislead ordinary souls), I should not want to blame them or to pass unfavorable judgment on them. Everyone has his own share of good sense, especially in foreign, external, and indifferent things which (since they do not spring from our hearts and minds) are neither good nor evil in themselves; our hearts and minds alone are the producers of all good and of all evil: good, if our minds are good and if our affections are governed by pure intent; evil, if the affections are depraved through the injustice of the evil spirit. The thing that displeases me is the novelty of your outfit and the contempt which you display for common custom."

"The color," Panurge replied, "is a prop à propos. It is the same as the cloth on my desk, and, henceforth, I want to wear it so as to be able to consider my business from close at hand. Since I'm out of debt for once, you'll never see a more unpleasant person than I'm going to be, so help me God! Look at my spectacles. To see me coming, you would say, right off, that I was Friar Jean Bourgeois.[3] I think, in fact, that I'll preach the crusade again this year. May God keep my little balls from harm!

"Do you see this brown cloth?[4] You may believe me when I tell you that it possesses an occult property known only to a few people. I put it on only this morning, and already I'm ranting, panting, burning to be married, and to work like a brown devil on my wife, without having to

[3] **Jean Bourgeois** 15th century Franciscan preacher [4] **Brown cloth** of a monk's habit

be afraid of a clubbing. Oh! the fine husband I'll be! After
my death, they'll burn me on an honorific pyre so that
they can keep my ashes in memory of the perfect husband.
By God, my treasurer is not going to play at changing
cents into dollars on my brown cloth, or he'll get my fists
in his face! Look at me before and behind: my coat is in
the form of a toga, the ancient dress of the Romans in
time of peace. I discovered its shape on Trajan's Column
in Rome, as well as on the triumphal Arch of Septimius
Severus.[5] I'm tired of war, tired of the soldier's cloak. My
shoulders are worn out from bearing armor. Let arms
cease and togas reign, at least for the coming year, that is,
if I should get married, as you explained yesterday, according to the Mosaic law.[6]

"As for my breeches, my great aunt Laurence used to
tell me that they were made for the codpiece. I believe
it, inducing it in the same way as good old Galen who
says, *lib. ix, On the Usage of our Members,*[7] that the head
is made for the eyes. For Nature might have put our heads
in our knees or elbows. But since eyes were ordained for
seeing at a distance, she fixed them in the head, as on
a pole, which is the highest part of the body, just as light-
houses and high towers are erected at seaports so that
their lantern can see far off.

"And since I should like to take a rest from the art of
war, for a year at least; that is, since I should like to get
married, I am no longer wearing a codpiece, and, consequently, no breeches. For the codpiece is the first piece
of armor a soldier puts on. And I maintain—and I'll go
as far as the fire to prove it—that the Turks are not
properly armed since they are forbidden by their law to
wear codpieces."

[5] both **Trajan's Column** and the **Arch of Septimius Severus** are
in the Forum   [6] **Mosaic Law** excused husbands from military
service during the first year of marriage   [7] Rabelais has erred;
the reference should be to Book VIII

How Panurge Asks Advice of Pantagruel as to Whether he Should Marry

Since Pantagruel did not say anything, Panurge continued, remarking with a profound sigh:

"Sir, you have heard my decision to get married—if it's not my luck to find all the holes shut, locked, and sealed—and I now implore you, by the love which you have had for me for so long, to tell me what you think of the whole thing."

"Since you have already cast the die," Pantagruel replied, "and have decreed it thus and taken a firm stand in the matter, there is no reason to talk about it any longer. The only thing for you to do is to carry out your decision."

"Yes," said Panurge, "but I don't want to carry it out without your advice and counsel."

"My counsel and advice," replied Pantagruel, "is for you to go ahead."

"But," said Panurge, "if you thought it would be better for me to remain as I am, without undertaking something new, I'd prefer not to marry."

"Prefer not to marry then," replied Pantagruel.

"Yes, but," said Panurge, "would you want me to remain all alone my whole life, without a conjugal companion? You know that it's written *Vae soli!* [1] A single man doesn't have the pleasure and joy of married people."

"Get married then, by God!" Pantagruel replied.

"But," said Panurge, "if my wife should make me a cuckold—for, as you know, this is a good year for them— this would be enough to unhinge my patience. I like cuckolds. They seem to me to be fine fellows, and I don't mind being with them; but I'd rather die than be one of them! That's a point which pricks me too much."

"Then make it a point not to get married," replied

[1] *Vae soli* Woe to him who is alone (*Ecclesiastes*)

Pantagruel, "for Seneca's maxim holds true without exception: what you do to others, be sure that others will do to you."

"Do you mean to say," asked Panurge, "that this is a rule without exception?"

"Without exception, or so he says," replied Pantagruel.

"Ho, ho!" said Panurge, "by my pet devil! Does he mean in this world, or in the other? But look here. Since I can't get along without a woman any more than a blind man can without a cane (for my gimlet must drill or I cannot live), is it not better for me to associate myself with some decent, honest woman, than to change every day and live in perpetual danger of being clubbed, or of catching the pox? For I've never yet found a good married woman—begging their husbands' pardons."

"Get married then, by God!" replied Pantagruel.

"But," said Panurge, "if God willed it, and if it so happened that I married some good woman who beat me, I'd have to have more than two-thirds of Job's patience not to go stark raving mad. They say that these good women are often headstrong, and, therefore, never without vinegar in the house. I'd go her one better and beat her giblets so, that is her arms, legs, head, lungs, liver, spleen, and so tear her clothing with repeated poundings, that the Devil himself would stand at the door waiting for her damned soul. I could get along very well without this kind of fracas for a year, and I'd be just as happy not to get into one."

"Then don't get into marriage," replied Pantagruel.

"Yes," said Panurge, "but being in the state I'm in, without debts and unmarried—and note that I say without debts sadly; for, if I were heavily in debt, my creditors would be only too concerned about my paternity—but, being out of debt and unmarried, I have no one to take care of me or to bring me that love they call conjugal. And if I should happen to fall ill, I'd only be mistreated. The wise man says: where there is no woman (and I take that to mean the mother of a family, in lawful wedlock), the sick man is in great misery. I've seen ample proof of this in the case of popes, legates, cardinals, bishops, abbots, priors, priests, and monks. No, you'll never get me in that state!"

"Then choose the state of matrimony, by God!" replied Pantagruel.

"But," said Panurge, "suppose that my wife, if I should become ill and be unable to perform my marital duties, impatient at my lassitude, should give herself to another man, failing me not only in my need, but even making fun of me in my distress, or (which is worse) robbing me, as I have often seen happen—that would really polish me off and make me run amuck."

"Don't run into marriage then," replied Pantagruel.

"But," said Panurge, "how else can I have legitimate sons and daughters? How else can I hope to perpetuate my name and arms? To whom can I leave my goods and possessions? (And I'm sure to have fine ones, someday, just you wait and see; moreover, I'll have vast sums to leave them). Who will bring me joy in my old age as you do every day to your kind and gentle father, and as children do to all decent people in their domestic and private lives? For being out of debt, being unmarried, being, as it so happens, worried, instead of consolation for my troubles, all I get from you is laughter."

"Console yourself then, by God, in marriage," replied Pantagruel.

How Pantagruel Persuaded Panurge to Seek Counsel of a Fool

Pantagruel, on his way to bed, noticed that Panurge was in the gallery looking like a dreamer, dreaming and nodding his head, and he said to him: "You remind me of a mouse caught in a trap. The more it tries to extricate itself, the more hopelessly entangled it becomes. You, likewise, trying to escape from the snares of perplexity, find yourself more entangled than ever before. I know of only one remedy. Listen. I have often heard the popular saying that a fool can teach a wise man a thing or two. Since you are not fully satisfied with the replies of wise men, consult some fool. Perhaps, in so doing, you will be satisfied in a way more to your liking. On the advice, counsel, and predictions of fools, you yourself know how many princes, kings, and republics have been preserved, how many battles won, how many perplexities resolved. There is no need to remind you of examples. You will agree with me in this definition: he who looks carefully after his private and domestic affairs, who is vigilant and attentive in the management of his household, whose mind does not wander, who loses no opportunity to acquire and amass goods and riches, who understands thoroughly how to avoid the inconveniences of poverty, such a one is wise in the eyes of the world. Yet he may be nothing more than an ass in the estimation of the Celestial Intelligences. In order to be wise in their opinion, that is, to be a sage capable of presaging by divine inspiration, of receiving the gift of divination, one must be able to forget one's self, to discard one's self, to empty one's senses of every human care, and to accept everything with indifference. These qualities are popularly associated with insanity. For this reason, the great soothsayer Faunus, son of Picus, King of the Latins, was called Fatuous[1] by the unexperienced common people. For this reason as well, we see that when roles are distributed to mummers, the Fool and the Jester are always played by the most talented and experienced actors of the group. And for this reason, mathematicians declare that kings and fools have the same horoscope at their birth. They cite the example of Aeneas and Choroebus,[2] considered a fool by Euphorion,[3] both of whom had the same horoscope.

"It is not inappropriate to tell you what Giovanni

[1] **Fatuous** from the Latin *fatuus*, meaning divine and stupid
[2] **Choroebus** son of King Mygdon the Phrygian who lost his senses at birth   [3] **Euphorion** according to Servius' *Commentary on the Aeneid*, II, 341

Andrea[4] said in a comment on the canon of a certain Papal writ addressed to the mayor and townspeople of La Rochelle, and, after him, Panormitanus[5] on the subject of the same canon, Barbatias[6] on the *Pandects,* and, recently, Jason[7] in his *Consilia,* concerning Lord John, famed fool of Paris, and Caillette's[8] great-grandfather. Here is his story:

"In Paris, one day, a porter was standing in front of the cookshop near the Petit Châtelet[9] eating his bread with the fumes emanating from the roast, and he found it to have a marvelous flavor when perfumed in this way. The cook did not interfere until the porter had gulped down all his bread. He then grabbed him by the collar, and insisted that he pay for the fumes from his roast. The porter maintained that he had not damaged his meat in any way, that he had taken nothing from him, and that he was not indebted to him in any way whatsoever. The fumes in question were evaporating in the air and would have been lost in any event. Never had he heard of anyone trying to sell fumes from a roast in the streets of Paris.

"The cook replied that the fumes of his roast were not for feeding porters, and he swore that if he did not pay him for them that he would take away the hooks he needed for carrying things.

"The porter drew out his club and prepared to defend himself. A great altercation ensued. The rubber-necked people of Paris rushed up from everywhere to witness the dispute. Appropriately enough, Lord John the Fool, citizen of Paris, was there. Spotting him, the cook asked the porter: 'Will you accept our noble Lord John's judgment of our disagreement?' 'Yes, by God,' said the porter.

"When Lord John had heard their pleas, he ordered the porter to produce a coin from his belt. The porter handed him a Philip[10] penny. Lord John took it, put it

[4] **Giovanni Andrea** 15th century Italian glossarist [5] **Panormitanus** 15th century Italian jurisconsult [6] **Barbatias** 15th century Italian jurisconsult [7] **Jason** 15th century Italian jurisconsult [8] **Caillette** was Louis XII's jester [9] **Petit Châtelet** prison in Paris [10] **Philip** ancient coin with effigy of Philip V of France

on his left shoulder as though checking its weight; then
he made it ring in the palm of his left hand as though
attempting to see if it were genuine; then he placed it on
his right eye as though to see if it were properly struck.
All this was done amid a great silence: the rubber-necks
watched curiously, the cook waited confidently, the porter
in despair. Then Lord John made the coin ring several
times on the counter, and, with presidential majesty, holding his jester's wand as if it were a scepter, and putting on
his cap of simulated fur, ridged like organ pipes, coughing
two or three good times as a preliminary, he proclaimed
in a loud voice: 'The court decrees that the porter, who has
eaten his bread by the fumes of the roast, has duly payed
the cook with the sound of his money. The said court
orders each and everyone to return to his own home, without charges. Case dismissed.' This decision handed down
by the Paris fool seemed so equitable, admirable, just, to
the above mentioned doctors, that they doubted that the
case, had it been placed before the Parliament of Paris,
or the Rota[11] of Rome, or the Areopagites[12] of Athens,
would have been any more judiciously settled by them.
If you want counsel, therefore, I advise you to consult a
fool."

How Panurge Consulted Triboulet

Six days later, Pantagruel arrived home at the very
same moment that Triboulet arrived by water from Blois.
Panurge presented him with a pig's bladder filled with air
and resonant with the dried peas he had put inside; with
a wooden sword, nicely gilt; with a small pouch made
from a turtle's shell; with a wicker-covered bottle filled
with Breton wine, and a quarter of Blandureau[1] apples.

"Why," said Carpalim, "he's as crazy as a garden cabbage!"

---

[11] **Rota** highest ecclesiastical court   [12] **Areopagites** supreme tri-
bunal of ancient Athens   [1] **Blandureau** a sweet, white variety

Triboulet girded on his sword and pouch, took the bladder in his hand, ate part of the apples, drank all the wine. Panurge watched him attentively, and said: "Never have I seen a fool—and I've seen more than ten thousand francs worth—who drank more heartily or deeper." He then proceeded to explain his problem in the most elegant rhetoric.

Before he had finished, Triboulet smacked him between the shoulders with his fist, handed him the bottle, hit him on the nose with the pig's bladder, and with a great shaking of the head, said only: "By God, God, crazy fool, beware the monk, Buzançay[2] bagpipe!" Having pronounced these words, he moved away from the group and played with his pig's bladder, delighting in the melodious sound of the peas. It was impossible to get another syllable out of him. Every time Panurge tried to interrogate him further, Triboulet drew his wooden sword and tried to strike him with it.

"That's a fine thing, indeed," said Panurge. "And that's some reply! He's really crazy, you can't deny it; but the person who brought him here is crazier still, and I'm the craziest of all for having told him my problems."

"That's a stone thrown into my garden," [3] said Carpalim.

"Now without getting upset," said Pantagruel, "let's consider his words and gestures. I have noticed that they contain mysterious signs. The more I think of it, the less astonished I am that the Turks respect fools as mushafis[4] and prophets. Did you see how his head shook and rocked even before he opened his mouth to speak. By the teachings of the ancient philosophers, by the ceremonies of magicians, by the comments of legal experts, you can judge that this movement was brought on by the advent and inspiration of the prophetic spirit, which, entering suddenly into a weak and small substance (a small head, as you know, cannot contain a large brain) has shaken it

[2] **Buzançay** town near Châteauroux where bagpipes were made
[3] **Carpalim** says this because he was responsible for bringing Triboulet [4] **mushafis** commentators of the Koran

for the same reasons, according to doctors, that the human body is shaken, that is, in part, because of the weight and violent impetuosity of the load carried, and ín part because of the physical weakness of the carrying organ.

"You have a manifest example of this in those who, when fasting, are unable to carry in their hands a large beaker full of wine without trembling. The Pythian prophetess[5] prefigured this for us when, before replying for the oracle, she shook a branch of her domestic laurel.[6] By the same token, Lampridius[7] states that the Emperor Heliogabalus,[8] wishing to earn a reputation as a soothsayer, shook his head violently in public, at several festivals of the great Idol, along with the eunuchs. Plautus,[9] in his *Asinaria*,[10] declares that Saurias walked around wagging his head as though he were mad and out of his senses, terrifying everybody he met. And, elsewhere,[11] he explains that Charmides shook his head because he was in ecstacy.

"Catullus,[12] in his *Berecynthia et Atys*, tells how the Maenads, Bacchic women, priestesses of Bacchus, demented prophetesses, bearing ivy leaves in their hands, shook their heads. The gelded Gauls, priests of Cybele,[13] did the same thing when they celebrated their rites. This explains her name, for the ancient theologians tell us that $\kappa v \beta \acute{\iota} \sigma \theta \alpha \iota$ means to turn, twist, shake the head, and to get a stiff neck.

"Livy[14] wrote that, during the Bacchanals at Rome, men and women seemed to vaticinate as the result of a certain shaking and agitation of the body which they affected. The common voice of philosophers and the opinion of the people was that vaticination was never given by the heavens unless accompanied by fury and shaking of the

[5] Pythian prophetess at Delphi, priestess of Apollo [6] domestic laurel sacred to Apollo [7] Lampridius late Latin historian [8] Heliogabalus Roman emperor (218-222A.D.) [9] Plautus Latin comic poet (c. 254-184B.C.) [10] II, iii, v. 387 [11] Trinummus, V, ii, v. 1122 [12] Catullus Latin lyric poet (c. 87-54B.C.) [13] Cybele great nature goddess [14] Livy Roman historian (59B.C.-17A.D.)

body. This occurred not only when it was received, but also when it declared and manifested itself.

"Indeed, Julian, the famous jurist, when asked once if a slave was considered sane who, in the company of fanatic and furious people, talked and prophesized without shaking his head, replied that he should be considered sane.

"Do we not now see preceptors and pedagogues who shake the heads of their pupils (as you shake a pot, by its handles), tweaking and pulling their ears (which are, according to the teachings of Egyptian sages, the organ consecrated to the memory) so as to bring them back to their senses. For, very often, the schoolboy is lost in strange fancies and wild distractions, and must be brought back to proper and philosophical disciplines. Virgil confesses that this happened to him, and that he was shaken by Apollo Cynthius." [15]

How Pantagruel and Panurge Interpret Diversely Triboulet's Words

"He says that you are a fool. And what kind of a fool? A mad fool who, in his old age, wants to bind and enslave himself by marriage. He says to you: 'Beware of the monk!' By my honor, you will be made a cuckold by some monk. I pledge my honor, I have nothing greater to pledge, and would not have were I the sole and pacific ruler of Europe, Africa, and Asia. Notice to what extent I defer to our morosophe[1] Triboulet. The other oracles and responses signified merely that you would be a cuckold; but none specified who would make your wife an adultress and you a cuckold. Our noble Triboulet has named the culprit. And the cuckoldry will be infamous and flagrantly scandalous. Will you have your conjugal bed given over to incest and contaminated by monkery?

"He says, moreover, that you will be the bagpipe of

[15] *Eclogues*, VI, 3-4   [1] morosophe wise-fool

Buzançay, that is, you will be well horned and hornified. And just as the man who was to ask Louis XII to give the revenue from the salt tax at Buzançay to his brother, asked instead for a bagpipe, you, similarly, thinking that you are marrying an honorable and virtuous woman, will marry an imprudent woman, full of the wind of conceit, shrill and disagreeable, like a bagpipe.

"Consider as well that he hit you on the nose with a pig's bladder and smacked you on the back with his fist. That's a prediction that you will be beaten, led by the nose, and robbed by your wife, just as you robbed the children of Vaubreton[2] of that pig's bladder."

"On the contrary," Panurge replied. "Not that I am presumptuous enough to want to exclude myself from the territory of foolishness. I'm a part of it, I admit it. Everyone is a fool. In Lorraine, Fool is quite rightly near Toul, which means 'all.' All are fools. Solomon says that the number of fools is infinite. Nothing can be subtracted or added to infinity, as Aristotle has proved. And I'd be a mad fool if, being a fool, I did not consider myself a fool. This is precisely what makes the number of maniacs and lunatics infinite. Avicenna[3] says that the kinds of madness are infinite.

"But the rest of his sayings and gestures are in my favor. He says to my wife: 'Beware of the monk!' He means a monkey that she'll be fond of, as Catullus shows Lesbia to be fond of a pet, which will chase flies and spend its time at this every bit as happily as Domitian the fly-cather did.[4]

"He says as well that she will be from a village, and as pleasant as a fine bagpipe from Saulieu or Buzançay. In truth, Triboulet recognized my natural inclinations and inward feelings; for I swear to you that I prefer a happy, dishevelled shepherdess whose arse smells of clover, to your ladies of the court with their rich finery and heady

---

[2] **Vaubreton** town near Chinon   [3] **Avicenna** Arab philosopher (980-1037)   [4] Anecdote recounted by Erasmus, *Adages*, II, i, 84

perfumes. Better the sound of the rustic bagpipe than the squeaking of lutes, rebecks, and court violins.

"He gave me a smack on my back. Well, what about it! Let it be, for the love of God, and count it as an installment on those I shall receive in Purgatory. He didn't do it with evil intentions. He thought he was striking some court page. He's an honest fool, an innocent fool, I assure you. He sins who thinks ill of him.

"He tweaked me on the nose? That symbolized the little frolics my wife and I will engage in, like any newly married couple."

How Pantagruel and Panurge Decided to Visit the Oracle of the Holy Bottle

"Here is another point you have not considered," Panurge went on. And it is, nevertheless, the heart of the matter. He handed me this bottle. What does that signify? What does that mean?"

"Maybe," replied Pantagruel, "it means that your wife will be a drunkard."

"On the contrary," said Panurge, "for the bottle was empty. I swear by the spine of St. Fiacre in Brie[1] that our morosophe, the unique, not lunatic Triboulet, sends me back to the bottle. And I renew once again my first vow, and swear by the Styx and Acheron,[2] in your presence, to wear glasses on my bonnet, not to wear a codpiece or my breeches until I have had the pronouncement of the Holy Bottle on my undertaking. I know a wise man, a friend of mine, who is familiar with the place, land, and country in which its temple and oracle are found. He will certainly lead us there. Let's all go together. I implore you not to refuse. I'll be an Achates[3] to you, a Damis,[4] a companion throughout the voyage. I've known you to be

---

[1] This relic was venerated in the cathedral at Meaux   [2] **Styx** and **Acheron** rivers of Hades   [3] **Achates** Aeneas's faithful companion   [4] **Damis** companion of Apollonius of Tyana, Greek Neo-Pythagorean philosopher

interested in peregrinations for a long time, and I realize that you enjoy seeing new things and learning about them. We shall see marvelous things, you can believe me!"

"I'm willing," replied Pantagruel. "But before starting off on a long journey, fraught with hazards and obvious dangers . . ."

"What dangers?" interrupted Panurge. "Dangers flee from me wherever I go, seven leagues around, just as a deputy retires when the king appears, just as shadows dissolve when the sun comes out, just as diseases vanish before St. Martin's body at Candes." [5]

"Incidentally," said Pantagruel, "before we set out, there are certain things we must settle. First of all, we must send Triboulet back to Blois (this was done immediately, and Pantagruel gave him a gold-embroidered coat). Secondly, we must have the advice and permission of the King, my father. And furthermore, we shall have to find some sibyl to act as guide and interpreter."

Panurge replied that his friend Xenomanes[6] would do quite well, and, moreover, he was planning to go through Lanternland, where they could choose some wise and learned lantern who would be for them during the voyage what the Sibyl was for Aeneas in his descent to the Elysian Fields. Carpalim, who was preparing to take Triboulet back, heard this proposal, and shouted: "Panurge, ho! Master Out-of-Debt, take Milord Debty at Calais along. He is a fine candle, and don't forget the debtors, that is, the lanterns. In this way, you'll have both candles and lanterns." [7]

"It is my prediction," said Pantagruel, "that we won't engender melancholy along the way. I can see this very clearly. I'm only sorry I don't speak good Lanternese."

"I'll speak it for all of you," said Panurge. "I understand it as well as I do my mother tongue. Why, it's as familiar to me as French. Listen:

[5] **Candes** near Chinon   [6] **Xenomanes** means Lover of Foreign Things   [7] **Milord Debty** *i.e.* Lord Deputy of Calais, then an English city. Involved and obscene play on words follows

Briszmarg d'algotbric nubstzne zos
Isquebfz prusq; alborlz crinqs zacbac.
Misbe dilbarlkz morp nipp stancz bos.
Strombtz Panrge walmap quost grufz bac.[8]

Guess what that means, Epistemon."

"Those are names of arrant, passant, and rampant devils," said Epistemon.

"Your words, my fine friend, are true," said Panurge, "though mine were in the courtly Lanternese language. I'll make you a nice little dictionary during the trip which will last you about as long as a pair of new shoes. You'll have learned it before you see the next dawn. What I said, translated from Lanternese into French, is the following:

Every distress, without a nest,
Haunted me—I knew only hell.
Married people are happiest.
Panurge is, and knows it well.

"All we need now," cried Pantagruel, "is to find out what the pleasure of the King, my father, will be, and to obtain his permission."

[8] gibberish of Rabelais's invention

THE FOURTH BOOK

❦

Of the Heroic Deeds and Sayings
of the Worthy Pantagruel

COMPOSED BY
M. FRANÇOIS RABELAIS
DOCTOR OF MEDICINE

How Pantagruel Put Out to Sea to Visit the Oracle of the Holy Bacbuc[1]

In the month of June, on the day of the Feast of Vesta[2] —the very day on which Brutus conquered Spain and subjugated the Spaniards, on which, also, Crassus the Avaricious was defeated and vanquished by the Parthians —Pantagruel, taking leave of good Gargantua, his father, who prayed (as was the laudable custom among the Christian saints of the early church) for a happy voyage for his son and all his company, put out to sea from the port of Thalasse.[3] He was accompanied by Panurge, Friar John Chopper, Epistemon, Gymnaste, Eusthenes, Rhizotome, Carpalim, and other servants and domestics, together with Xenomanes, the great traveller and traverser of perilous ways, who had arrived a few days before at Panurge's request. For certain very good reasons, Xenomanes had plotted with Gargantua, on his vast and universal hydrography,[4] the route they were to take in order to visit the oracle of the Holy Bottle Bacbuc.

I already indicated the number of ships in the Third

[1] **Bacbuc** Rabelais informs the reader that this is the Hebrew word for bottle, so called because of the sound it makes when emptied [2] **Feast of Vesta** June 9 [3] **Thalasse** means Sea in Greek [4] **hydrography** marine map

Book, and they were escorted by an equal number of tiremes, long boats, galleons, and Liburnian[5] galleys, all well equipped, well calked, well provisioned with a good store of Pantagruelion.[6] The officers, interpreters, pilots, captains, seamen, cabin-boys, rowers, and sailors assembled on the Thalanege.[7] This was the name of Pantagruel's flagship, and it had on its poop, as an ensign, a large and capacious bottle, half smooth and polished silver, and half gold, enamelled a carnation hue. One could readily see from this that white and red were the colors of our noble travellers, and that they were off to seek the word of the Bottle.

An antique lantern was set up on the poop of the second ship. It was fashioned skilfully of transparent phengites stone, and denoted that they were to pass through Lantern country.

The ensign of the third ship was a fine deep porcelain bowl.

The fourth, a golden pot with two handles, like an ancient urn.

The fifth, a distinguished looking pitcher of sperm-emerald.

The sixth, a monastic flagon made of four metals combined.

The seventh, an ebony funnel, embossed and inlaid with gold.

The eighth, a most precious ivy goblet, with damascene workmanship.

The ninth, a glass of refined gold.

The tenth, a cup of aromatic agalloche, a wood which you call aloes, incrusted with Cyprian gold thread in the Persian fashion.

The eleventh, a vintage-basket of gold mosaics.

[5] **Liburnian** name Romans gave their fastest ships   [6] **Pantagruelion** mysterious substance described in great detail at the end of the *Third Book*. Identified as hemp by some scholars   [7] **Thalanege** a ship with rooms. Most ancient ships had none

The twelfth, a wine cask of unpolished gold, covered with vignettes of huge Indian pearls and topiary[8] work.

Accordingly, there was no one, no matter how sad, angry, sour-faced, melancholy he might be—and this includes even Heraclitus the Weeper[9]—who would not have been filled with new joy, and who would not have smiled with pleasure at seeing this noble line of ships with all its ensigns. And there is no one who would not have said that these voyagers were all drinkers, good fellows, and who would not have prophesized with conviction that their voyage, both going and coming, would be accomplished in happiness and perfect health.

When they had all assembled on the Thalamege, Pantagruel made a brief and pious speech, based on sayings culled from Holy Scriptures, dealing with their journey. When he had finished, he prayed to God in a loud, clear voice, and his prayer was audible to the bourgeois and townspeople of Thalasse who had gathered on the quay to see them off.

After the prayer, they sang harmoniously the psalm of holy King David beginning, *When Israel Went out of Egypt*.[10] Once the psalm was finished, tables were set up on the deck, and food was served. The Thalassians, who had joined in singing the psalm, sent quantities of food and drink from their homes. Everybody drank to them. They drank to everybody. This explains why not a single member of the crew was seasick during the entire voyage, or suffered from any upset of stomach or head. Nor could they have avoided these inconveniences as readily by drinking sea water for a few days before sailing (either pure or mixed with wine), or by using quinces, lemon peel, bitter-sweet pomegranate juice, or by prolonged fasting, or by covering the stomach with paper, or by any of the other remedies which foolish doctors prescribe for those who go to sea.

[8] topiary set in floral patterns   [9] Heraclitus the Weeper Greek philosopher (576-480B.C.)   [10] *When . . . Egypt* vernacular versions of the psalms had been condemned by the Sorbonne

After repeated libations, each returned to his own ship. Soon they set sail with a fine wind from the east; the chief navigator, Jamet Brayer, had charted this route for them, and had set all the compass needles accordingly. It was his opinion, as well as that of Xenomanes, since the oracle of the Holy Bacbuc was near Cathay in Upper India, that they ought not to follow the route normally taken by the Portuguese which, crossing the torrid zone of the equator, skirting the Cape of Good Hope at the southern tip of Africa, losing sight of the Arctic Pole, necessitates a long voyage. Instead, they would follow more closely the parallel of India, swinging around the pole to the west, so that, coming in from the north, they would find themselves at the same latitude as the port of Olonne,[11] but without going any closer to it for fear of entering and being trapped in the Frozen Sea. According to this canonical detour by the parallel mentioned, they would have on their right, towards the east, what, on their departure, they had on their left. This proved advantageous; for, without shipwreck, without danger, without loss of crew, they sailed serenely (except for one day near the island of the Macreons)[12] all the way to Upper India, in less than four months. The Portuguese, on the other hand, can barely make this same voyage in three years, encountering a thousand accidents and innumerable dangers on the way.[13] It is my opinion (and will remain so until someone offers a better one) that this was probably the route taken by the Indians who sailed to Germany and who were honorably received by the King of the Suevians.[14] This took place when Q. Metellus Celer was

[11] **Olonne** port on west coast of France; now Les Sables d'Olonne [12] **Macreons** the Aged Folk   [13] the voyage in search of the Holy Bottle follows the route taken by Portuguese explorers to Cathay. The series of islands at which they call provides Rabelais with the opportunity of satirizing, in allegorical fashion, a number of abuses of the day   [14] **Suevians** ancient Germanic people, mentioned by Caesar as dwelling east of the Rhine

proconsul in Gaul, according to Cor. Nepos, Pomp. Mela, and Pliny.[15]

How Pantagruel Met a Ship Full of Travellers Returning From Lanternland

On the fifth day out, as we were already beginning to circle the pole and to move away gradually from the equinoctial line, we discovered a merchant ship off our port side. There was great rejoicing both by us and by the merchants: by us, hearing news of the sea; by them, hearing news of the land. Standing by, we realized that they were Frenchmen from Saintonge. In talking and discussing with them, Pantagruel learned that they were returning from Lanternland. Our happiness increased even more upon hearing this, as did that of the whole group, and we all inquired about the country and the customs of the Lantern people. We were told that a general council of Lanterns had been convened for the end of this coming July,[1] and that, if we were to arrive at that time (as we easily could), then we would see a fine, honorable, and joyous assemblage of Lanterns. They were making great preparations for it, as if they intended to lanternize profoundly. They told us as well that if we were to pass by Gebarim,[2] we would be magnificently received and treated by King Ohabe,[3] ruler of this land. He and all his subjects speak the French of Touraine.[4]

While we were listening to this news, Panurge was debating with a merchant from Taillebourg,[5] called Dindenault. This is how the quarrel started. Dindenault, noticing that Panurge was without a codpiece and that

[15] Cornelius Nepos, Roman biographer; Pomponius Mela, geographer; Pliny the Elder, naturalist   [1] probable allusion to the sixth session of the Council of Trent, held on July 29, 1546   [2] **Gebarim** name meaning Kingdom of Warriors in Hebrew   [3] **Ohabe** meaning My Friend, in Hebrew   [4] **Touraine** garden of France and province where the purest French is spoken   [5] **Taillebourg** village on the Charente, near Saintes

his spectacles were attached to his bonnet, said to one of his companions: "Here's a fine portrait of a cuckold." Panurge, thanks to his spectacles, heard more clearly than usual. Catching this remark, therefore, he inquired of the merchant:

"How in the devil can I be a cuckold since I'm not married yet, as you are, if I am to judge from your ungracious snout?"

"Yes, indeed," replied the merchant, "I am, and I wouldn't be unmarried for all the spectacles in Europe, or all the goggles of Africa. And I have married one of the most beautiful, most pleasing, most faithful, most discreet of women in the whole land of Saintonge[6]—with all due respect to the others. I'm bringing her back as a gift from my trip a fine branch of red coral, eleven inches long. What business is it of yours? What has it to do with you? Who are you? Where are you from? O optician of Antichrist, answer, if you are of God."

"I'm asking you," said Panurge, "if with the consent and concordance of all the elements I sackholepushdinglebanged your most beautiful, most pleasing, most faithful, most discreet of women, in such a way that the stiff god of gardens Priapus, which dwells here in liberty, unhampered by the subjection of a codpiece, got stuck in her and would remain there eternally if you did not pull it out with your teeth, what would you do? Would you leave it there forever, or would you pull it out with your teeth? Answer, ram of Mahomet, since you are of the devil."

"I'd strike you with my sword on that spectacle bearing ear," replied the merchant, "and I would kill you like a ram." So saying, he began to take out his sword. But it stuck in the scabbard, for, as you know, all armor rusts easily at sea because of the excessive and nitrous moisture. Panurge ran to Pantagruel for help. Friar John put his hand to his sword, freshly sharpened, and would have

[6] **Saintonge** province on the Bay of Biscay in which Taillebourg is located

killed the merchant if the owner of the ship and the passengers had not begged Pantagruel to prevent such a scandal from occurring on board. The quarrel was settled, and Panurge and the merchant shook hands, then drank merrily together in token of perfect reconciliation.

How Pantagruel Escaped from a Mighty Tempest at Sea

The next day, to starboard, we sighted nine vessels filled with monks—Dominicans, Jesuits, Capuchins, Hermits, Augustins, Bernardins, Celestins, Theatins, Egnatins, Anadeans, Franciscans, Carmelites, Minims,[1] and other sainted religious, all of whom were on their way to the Council of Chesil [2] to pick over the articles of faith which were to be issued against the new heretics.[3] Upon seeing them, Panurge was overjoyed; he felt sure of good luck that day, and many more to follow. He greeted the blessed fathers courteously, commending the salvation of his soul to their devout prayers and acts of piety, and then proceeded to load on their ships seventy-eight dozen hams, a quantity of caviar, Bologna sausages by the tens, Provençal caviar by the hundreds, and two thousand five gold angels[4] for the souls of the departed.

Pantagruel stood by, pensive and melancholy. Friar John noticed this, and was just about to ask him the reason for this unusual depression when the pilot, viewing the flapping of the ensign above the poop and predicting a fierce wind and sudden storm, ordered that everybody be put on a state of alert—seamen, sailors, stewards, as well as we passengers. The sails were lowered, mizzen, spanker, topsails, lug, mainsail, and bowsprit; the small sail and the main topsail were hauled in, the main mizzen sail was run down, and only the yards and the shrouds were left.

[1] All these orders actually exist [2] **Chesil** means Madman in Hebrew [3] **new heretics** Rabelais is alluding to the Council of Trent [4] **gold angels** coin with St. Michael imprint

Suddenly the sea began to swell and rise up from its lowest depths, and huge waves began to beat against the sides of our ships; a nor'wester arose, bringing with it an unbridled hurricane, black clouds, terrible rushing winds, and deadly squalls which roared through our rigging. Down from the heavens came thunder, lightning, rain, hail. The air lost its transparency and became opaque, dark, and ominous, save when the lightning flashed and zigzag streaks of fire rent the clouds. Everything around us, rain, wind, squall, and raging seas, flashed and flamed with lightning bolts and other ethereal explosions. Our faces were grim and desperate as the furious typhoon raised up mountainous waves from the deep. You may well believe that we imagined this to be exactly like primitive chaos in which fire, air, sea, and earth, all the elements, clashed in rebellious confusion.

Panurge fed the scatophagic[5] fishes plentifully from the contents of his stomach, and hugged the deck in distress, down-hearted, and half dead. He called all the blessed male and female saints to his aid, promised to go to confession as soon as time and place allowed, and cried out in great terror, saying: Steward, ho, my friend, my father, my uncle, bring me a bit of salt meat. We are going to have our fill of water from what I can see. Eat little, drink much will be my motto from now on. Would to God, to the blessed, worthy, and sacred Virgin, that I were on dry land at this very moment, all nice and comfortable!

"Thrice and four times happy are they who plant cabbages! O Fates, why did you not destine me to plant cabbages! Oh, how few in number are those whom Jupiter has so favored that he destined them to plant cabbages! They always have one foot on the ground, and the other one not far off! Talk about happiness and highest good all you want—anyone who plants cabbage is now declared by my edict most happy. And I have a better rea-

---

[5] **scatophagic** ordure-eating

son for asserting this than Pyrrho[6] did when, in danger much like ours, seeing a hog munching barley which had been scattered along the shore, he declared it most happy on two accounts: first, because it had lots of barley, and secondly, because it was on dry land.

"Ha! for a godly and lordly manor, there is nothing like a cowshed! This wave is going to sweep us away, God, save us! O my friends, a drop of vinegar. I'm sweating in great anguish. Alas, the yard-arm gears are broken, the ropes are in shreds, the rings are bursting, the lookout-mast has fallen into the sea, the keel is as high as the sun, our cables have almost all snapped. Alas, alas! where are our small sails? All is lost, by God. Our mizzen mast is in the water. Alas! who will claim this wreck? Friends, carry me to the shelter of the sterncastle. Your lantern fell, lads. Alas! don't give up the rudder or the tackle. I can hear the pintle cracking. Is it broken? For God's sake, save the rigging—don't bother about the oarlocks. Baa, baa, baa, boo, boo! Check the needle of your compass, I beg you, Master Astrophile;[7] see where this storm is coming from. Good God, I'm scared. Buh, buh, buh, bus, bus, bus. I'm dead and gone. I'm beshitting myself, I'm so afraid. Buh, buh, buh, buh! Otto to to to to ti! Otto to to to to ti! Buh, buh, bhu, ou ou ou bou bou bous bous. I'm drowning, I'm drowning, I'm dying! Mates, I'm drowning!"

End of the Tempest

"Land, land," cried Pantagruel, "I see land! Lads, take heart, we are not far from port. I see the sky clearing on the north. Look to the southeast!"

"Courage, lads," said the pilot, "the swell is falling. To the maintop. Hoist, hoist! To the aftermizzen. The bowlines! Pull, pull, pull. The halyard. Hoist, hoist, hoist. Bring 'er about. Ready tackle. Clear your sheets. Clear

[6] **Pyrrho** Greek skeptic (360-270B.C.) [7] **Astrophile** means Friend of the Stars.

your bowlines. To port. Bring the helm into the wind. Slack, to starboard, you son of a bitch!"

"You must be pleased, my friend," said Friar John, "to hear news of your mother!"

"Luff, put 'er into the wind."

"Keep 'er up! Helm up."

"It's up," said a sailor.

"Head her towards port. Attach the studding-sails. Hoist, hoist."

"Well said and done," Friar John exclaimed. "Pull, pull, pull, lads, go to it. Good. Hoist, hoist."

"To starboard."

"Well said and done. The storm is at its peak and will soon blow over. Thank God for that. The devils that plagued us are beginning to flee."

"Out with your sails!"

"Well and wisely said. Sails, sails. This way, by God, buddy Ponocrates, lusty rascal! He'll breed only boys, the fornicator. Euthenes, my lad, up the fore-topsail!"

"Hoist, hoist!"

"Well said. Hoist, by God, hoist, hoist!"

"I'm not going to be afraid of anything, for this is a holiday. Hurrah! Hurrah! Hurrah!"

"This song of cheer," said Epistemon, "is perfectly in season. This is a day for celebrating."

"Hoist, hoist, good!"

"Oh," cried Epistemon, "everything is going to be all right. I can see Castor, off to starboard."

"Baa, baa, bous, bous, bous," Panurge said. "I'm only afraid that it may be that bitch Helen." [1]

"It's actually Mixarchigevas," [2] Epistemon replied, "if you want the Argive[3] name for it. Ahoy, ahoy, I see land, I see the shore, I see a great number of people in the harbor. I see a light on a obeliscolychnie." [4]

---

[1] **Helen** star considered bad luck by the Ancients   [2] **Mixarchigevas** Greek name for Castor   [3] **Argive** Greek   [4] **obeliscolychnie** lighthouse in the shape of an obelisk

"Ahoy, ahoy!" said the pilot, "double the cape and watch the shallows."

"It's doubled," replied the sailors.

"She's clear," said the pilot. "So are the other ships. Let's have a drink."

"By St. John," cried Panurge, "now you're talking. Ah, what a beautiful word!"

"Mmm, mmm, mmm," said Friar John, "if you touch a drop of this, may the Devil touch me. Do you hear, you devilish bastard? Here, friend, here's a tankard of the very best for you. Bring out the mugs, ho, Gymnastes, and that dog of a jam or ham pie, makes no difference which. Don't spill any."

"Courage," cried Pantagruel, "courage, lads. Let's be happy. Look here, near our ship. There are two skiffs, three sloops, five brigs, eight schooners, four clippers, and six frigates, all of which have been sent to our aid by the good people of this island. But who is that Ucalegon[5] over there moaning and complaining? Wasn't I holding the mast firmly in my hands, and even straighter than two hundred cables ever could?"

"It's that poor devil Panurge," replied Friar John. "He has calf's fever. He shakes from fright when he's drunk."

"To have been afraid during that horrible storm and perilous tempest was quite natural," said Pantagruel. "Had Panurge helped us in spite of his fear, I'd not respect him any less. But fear at the slightest bump is a sign of the common and cowardly heart. Because Agamemnon was ever fearful, Achilles reproached him ignominiously for his dog's eyes and doe's heart. By the same token, to be unafraid when there is an obvious cause for fear, is a sign of little or no common sense. Now, if there is something in this life to fear besides God, I wouldn't say that it was death. I have no desire to discuss, as Socrates and the Academics, whether death be evil or fearful in itself.

[5] **Ucalegon** name which means Not Helping. There is an old Trojan in the *Iliad* of this name

I mean only whether death by drowning is evil or fearful. For, as Homer says, it is a grave, horrifying, and unnatural thing to die at sea. In fact, Aeneas, during the storm which caught him and his convoy of ships near Sicily, regretted that he had not died at the hands of strong Diomedes,[6] and asserted that those who had died in the Trojan conflagration were thrice and four times blessed. But no one has died here, may God our Saviour be eternally praised for that. To be sure we are going to have a lot to do in order to get everything shipshape. We shall have to repair all this damage. Take care not to run 'er aground."

How, Once the Storm was Over, Panurge Acted Like a Good Fellow

"Ah, ha!" said Panurge, "everything's fine. The storm is over. Please be kind enough to let me disembark first. I have some very important business to attend to. Shall I give you a hand there? Let me help you with that rope. I have little fear and a great deal of courage. Hand me that, mate. No, no, not a speck of fear. It's true, that decuman[1] wave which swept over us from prow to poop made my heart skip a beat."

"Lower the sails!"

"Now you're talking. Ah, aren't you doing anything, Friar John? How do we know that St. Martin's flunkey[2] isn't stirring up another storm for us? Shall I help you there a bit? Good God! I'm sorry, but it's a little late, that I didn't follow the teaching of those good philosophers who say that to stroll by the sea and to sail by the land is a very safe and delightful thing, just as it is to ride while leading the horse by the bridle. Ha, ha, ha! By God, everything's fine! Would you like a little more help there? Pass me that. I'll do it, or may the devil take me."

Epistemon had one hand that was all raw and bleeding

[6] **Diomedes** one of bravest of the Greek warriors before Troy
[1] **decuman** the tenth one   [2] **St. Martin's flunkey** the Devil

from the cables he had held onto so hard. When he heard Panurge's words, he said: "Believe me, sir, when I say that I was as afraid and as terrified as Panurge. And so what? I didn't spare myself when it came to helping out. It's my opinion that if dying is (as, indeed, it is) necessarily fatal and inevitable, then dying at such and such an hour, or in such and such a way, is God's holy will. This is why we must constantly implore, invoke, pray, entreat, beg Him. But we should not stop there. We should also make an effort on our own, and, as the Holy Apostle says, cooperate with Him. You know what Caius Flaminus, the consul, said when Hannibal in his cleverness cornered him near the Perugian lake called Trasimenus.[3] "My lads," he said to his soldiers, "you must not count on vows and prayers to the gods to get you out of here. You will escape through strength and courage, and by cutting a path at sword's point through the thick of the enemy."

Sallust reports that Marcus Porcius Cato said [4] that the aid of the gods is not obtained through useless vows and womanish lamentations. Things are brought to a desired end and a happy conclusion through watching, working, exertion. If man is negligent and indolent when in need or danger, he implores the gods in vain; his pleas serve only to anger and to antagonize them.

"May the devil take me," said Friar John ("He has already taken half of you," interpolated Panurge), "if the devastation and destruction of the close of Seuilly wouldn't have been complete if I had done nothing but sing *contra hostium insidias*[5] (that's breviary stuff) along with the other monkish devils, and had not protected the vineyard with my staff of the cross from the pillagers of Lerné."

"Full steam ahead," said Panurge, "all's fine. Friar John isn't doing a thing there. His name should be Friar John Donothing. He just looks at me as I sweat here and slave to help this good man. Sailor, mate, ho! A word or two

---

[3] **Trasimenus** in central Italy (217B.C.)   [4] *Catilina*, I.ii, 29
[5] *contra . . . insidias* against the snares of the enemy

with you, if I may. How thick are the planks of this ship?"

"They are a good two inches thick," replied the pilot. "You don't have a thing to worry about there."

"Good God," said Panurge. "Are we always to be only two inches away from death? Is this one of the nine joys of marriage? Ha, mate, that's fine if you measure danger by the yardstick of fear. I have no fear myself. Fearless William[6] is my name. I've courage to spare. I don't mean sheep's courage, either, but the courage of a wolf, the nerve of a murderer. And I'm not afraid of anything except danger."

How Pantagruel Sailed by the Island of Dissimulation where Shrovetide Reigned

The ships of the joyous convoy were refitted and repaired, new stores were taken aboard, the Macraeons[1] were pleased and satisfied with Pantagruel's expenditures on the island, and our men were happier than usual. They set sail joyously on the following day with a brisk and favorable wind. Towards high noon, Xenomanes pointed out to us the Island of Dissimulation in the distance. This was where Shrovetide reigned. Pantagruel had heard about him before and was interested in seeing him in person. Xenomanes discouraged him from this, not only because it would have meant a detour, but also because pickings were slim on the whole island as well as at the court of its King. "All you'll see there for your money," he said, "is a big swallower of dried peas, a big mackerel-snatcher, an overgrown mole-cacher, a big hay-bundler, a half-giant with downy hair and a double tonsure, of Lanternese extraction, a great big lantern bearer, a gonfalonier of the Ichthyophages,[2] a dictator of Mustardland,[3] a flogger of little children, a calcinator of ashes, father and foster-child

---

[6] **Fearless William** hero of a medieval epic of the same name
[1] **Macraeons** inhabitants of the Macraeon Islands, the land of the Aged Folk [2] **Ichthyophages** Fish Eaters [3] **Mustardland** mustard was commonly used during Lent with fish

of doctors, swarming with pardons, indulgences and stations, a good man, good Catholic, and extremely devout. He weeps three-fourths of the day. He never goes to weddings. But he's the most industrious manufacturer of larding pins and skewers in forty kingdoms. About six years ago when I landed at Dissimulation Island, I picked up a gross of them for the butchers of Candé. They thought highly of them, and rightly so. I'll show you a pair of them when we get back, hung up on the main portal of the church.[4] And he feeds upon salted helmets, casks, salted morions, and salted sallets.[5] Such fare occasionally gives him a good case of hotpiddle. His clothing is merry in cut as well as in color: grey and cold, nothing fore and nothing aft, with sleeves to match."

"Now that you have described his clothing, food, behavior, and pastimes," said Pantagruel, "I'd be pleased to hear a description of his shape and form."

"Please do, my little ballock," said Friar John, "for I've found him in my breviary. He comes right after the movable feasts."

"I'd be very happy to," replied Xenomanes. "We'll probably hear more of him at Savage Island, the land of the plump chitterlings. They are his mortal enemies, and he wages sempiternal warfare against them. Were it not for the help of noble Mardigras, their protector and good neighbor, that big lantern bearing Shrovetide would have driven them out of their homes and exterminated them long ago."

"Are they male or female," asked Friar John, "angel or mortal, women or virgins?"

"They are female in sex, mortal in condition, some are virgins, others are not," replied Xenomanes.

"I'll be damned," said Friar John, "if I'm not on their side! What kind of perversion is this, making war against women! Let's go back. Let's chop this villain up into little pieces."

[4] The portal of the church at Candé (near Angers) is decorated with stone needles   [5] **sallets** helmets

"Fight Shrovetide?" said Panurge, "By all the devils, I'm not that mad, and I'm not that stupid. *Quid juris,*[6] if we found ourselves caught between Chitterlings and Shrovetide? Between the hammer and the anvil? A pox on you! Stay away from there! Let's sail on. Farewell, Shrovetide, I say. I recommend the Chitterlings to you, and don't forget the Blood Pudding Sausages.

How Pantagruel Landed on the Island of Ruach[1]

We arrived two days later at the Island of Ruach, and I swear by the Pleiades that I found the way and life of its people stranger than I can say. They live entirely from wind. Their houses are weathercocks. They sow only three kinds of anemones[2] in their gardens. They are careful to pick rue and all other similar carminative[3] herbs. The common people eat fans made out of feathers, of paper, of linen, according to their means and wealth. The rich live on windmills. They set up their tables under a windmill or two whenever they have a feast or a banquet, and they indulge themselves as merrily as you would at a wedding. And, as they eat, they discuss the body, excellence, salubrity, rarity of winds just as you, my drinking friends, philosophize over wines. One praises the sirocco, another the southwest wind; one prefers the southeast wind, another the north wind; one vaunts the zephyr or west wind, another the northwestern, and so on. The dandies and ladies' men like lingerie wind. They treat the sick with draughts, just as we give our sick draughts of medicine. "Oh!" said a little bloater, "where can I get a bladderful of that good Languedoc wind, the one called Circisis?[4] The famous doctor Scurron[5] told us once when

[6] *Quid juris* What decision of law   [1] **Ruach** Wind, in Hebrew   [2] **anemones** the word means wind in Greek   [3] **carminative** means for flatulence or excess gas   [4] **Circisis** west-northwest wind, called Circius by the Ancients   [5] **Scurron** was a physician Rabelais knew when he was at the University of Montpellier

he was in this country that it is so strong that it overturns loaded wagons. Oh, it would do my oedipodic leg[6] a lot of good! The biggest are not the best."

"But," said Panurge, "what is better than a big butt of that good Languedoc wine which grows at Mirevaux, Canteperdris and Frontignan?" [7]

"I saw a fine looking man, dropsical in appearance, who was greatly enraged at a big fat servant and a little page. He was kicking them like the devil. Not knowing the cause of this anger, I assumed that he was following his physician's advice; it's a healthy thing for a master to become angry and to beat his servants, just as it is a healthy thing for a servant to be beaten. But then I heard him reproach his servants for robbing him of half a bagful of southwesterly wind which he had stored away lovingly, as a rare treat for late autumn. They do not spit, shit, or piss on this island. But they do break wind, fart, and belch copiously. They suffer every sort and kind of illness. And every illness springs and proceeds from ventosity, as Hippocrates shows in his *Lib. de Flatibus*.[8] Their worst epidemic is wind colic. As a remedy, they use large sucking-cups into which they blow veritable gales of wind. They all die of dropsy and tympanites.[9] And the men die farting, the women breaking wind. And their soul leaves the body through their arse.

Later, while strolling about the island, we met three great windbags, who were off to amuse themselves by watching plovers,[10] which abound there and which live on wind. I noticed that just as we drinkers, when we stroll about the country, carry flasks, bottles, flagons, so each of them carried a nice little bellows at his belt. If by chance the wind failed them, they could produce fresh ones by attraction and reciprocal expulsion of these nice bellows,

[6] **oedipodic leg** like Oedipus, who had swollen ankles   [7] **Mirevaux . . . Frontignan** three famous wines   [8] *Lib. de Flatibus* Book on Gas   [9] **tympanites** swelling of the abdomen caused by air in the intestine   [10] **plovers** birds which were supposed to live on wind

for, as you know, wind is essentially nothing but floating and undulating air.

At this moment, we received a command from their king not to permit on our ships for three hours any man or woman from the island. Somebody had robbed him of a full-bodied fart which that good snorer Aeolus[11] had given Ulysses to use when his ships were becalmed. He had kept it religiously, like another Holy Grail, and had cured several grave illnesses with it merely by letting loose and distributing to patients as much of it as would go into a virginal fart—which is what our Sanctimoniales[12] call sonnets.[13]

How Pantagruel Landed on the Island of the Papimaniacs

Leaving behind the desolate Island of the Popefiggers,[1] we sailed very serenely and pleasantly for a day, and then the blessed Island of the Papimaniacs[2] came into view. As soon as we had dropped anchor in the harbor, and even before we could fasten our moorings, we were approached by a skiff containing four persons diversely garbed. One was befrocked, bedraggled, booted like a monk. The second was clad like a falconer, with a lure and a bird-glove. The third as a trial lawyer, with a big bag full of briefs, citations, chicanery, and postponements in his hand. The fourth, like an Orléanais vintner, with handsome linen gaiters, a large basket, and a pruning knife at his belt.

As soon as they had come aboard, they cried out all together in a loud voice:

"Have you seen him, good travellers? Have you seen him?"

"Who?" Pantagruel asked.

"Him," they replied.

[11] **Aeolus** god of winds   [12] **Sanctimoniales** Nuns   [13] **sonnets** play on words since "sonnet" means little sound   [1] **Popefiggers** those who thumb their nose at the Pope   [2] **Papimaniacs** those who are infatuated with the Pope

"Who is Him?" Friar John asked. "By God, I'll trounce him for you." For he thought they were inquiring after some thief, murderer, or sacrilegious wretch.

"What, don't you know the One and Only, strangers?" they asked.

"Gentlemen," said Epistemon, "we don't understand your terms. But explain to us, if you will, what you mean, and we'll tell you the whole truth."

"We are talking about he who is," they said. "Have you never seen him?"

"He who is," replied Pantagruel, "according to our theological doctrine, is God. This is how he declared Himself to Moses. Of course we have never seen Him, nor is He visible to mortal eyes."

"We aren't talking about that God on high who rules in heaven," they said. "We are talking about the God on earth. Have you never seen him?"

"They mean the pope, I swear they do," said Carpalim.

"Yes, yes," replied Panurge, "indeed, gentlemen, I've seen three of them. But I'm not much better off for it."

"What!" they exclaimed. "Our sacred *Decretals*[3] proclaim that there is only one living at a time."

"I mean," Panurge explained, "that I saw them successively, one after the other. I only saw one at a time in a word."

"O thrice and four times happy people," they said. "You are welcome, and more than welcome!"

They then got down on their knees before us and tried to kiss our feet. We stopped them, however, pointing out that if ever the Pope were to come in person, they could not do him greater homage. "Yes, yes, we could," they replied. "We have already decided what to do. We would kiss his bare arse, and his balls as well. For the Holy Father has balls; our fair *Decretals* tell us so. Otherwise he couldn't be Pope. Thus, according to our subtle decretaline philosophy, this is a necessary consequence: he is

---

[3] *Decretals* collection of papal laws and decisions

Pope, therefore he has balls; when there are no more balls in the world, there will be no more Popes."

Pantagruel, meanwhile, asked a cabin boy on their skiff who these people were. He replied that they represented the Four Estates of the island.[4] He added that we would be well received and treated since we had seen the Pope. Pantagruel told this to Panurge, who whispered to him: "I swear to God, that's it. Everything comes to him who waits. We never got anything before for seeing the Pope, and now, by all the devils in hell, we're going to get something out of it!"

Then we disembarked, and the whole population of the country came to meet us in procession, men, women, little children. Our Four Estates said to them in a loud voice: "They have seen him! They have seen him! They have seen him!"

At this proclamation, they all got down on their knees, raised their hands towards heaven, and shouted: "O blessed ones! O fortunate ones!" And this acclamation lasted a quarter of an hour. Then the schoolmaster came running up with all his pedagogues, pupils, and students, and he flogged them magisterially, just as the children in our country are flogged when a criminal is hanged so as to impress it in their memory. Pantagruel was irritated at this, and said to them: "Gentlemen, if you do not stop beating these children, I shall leave." The people were astonished upon hearing his stentorian voice, and I overheard a little hunchback with long fingers ask the schoolmaster: "By the *Extravagantes*,[5] do people who see the Pope become as tall as the person who just threatened us? Oh, I can hardly wait to see him so that I can grow and become as tall as that."

Their exclamations were so loud that Homenas[6] (as they

---

[4] **Four Estates** the monk represents the Clergy; the falconer, the Nobility; the lawyer, the Bourgeoisie; the vintner, the People [5] *Extravagantes* is the name given to the Supplement of the *Decretals* [6] **Homenas** Langue d'Oc for big, strong, and stupid man.

called their bishop) hastened to meet them. He was on an unbridled mule with green trappings and was attended by his vassals (as he called them) and his vessels as well: crosses, banners, gonfalons, baldachins,[7] torches, holy water founts.

And he wanted desperately to kiss our feet (as the good Christian Valfinier[8] kissed Pope Clement's). He quoted one of their hypophetes,[9] a scourer and commentator of their holy *Decretals*, as saying that just as the Messiah finally came to the Jews who had long awaited him, so, too, one day the Pope would come to this island. Until this blessed time, should any one land here who had seen him at Rome or elsewhere, he was assured of being feasted and treated reverently.

Nevertheless, we excused ourselves courteously.

How, on the High Seas, Pantagruel Heard Various Thawed Words

On the high seas, once more, we were banqueting, nibbling, chatting, and having a merry discussion. Suddenly, Pantagruel got up and looked all around. Then he said to us: "Don't you hear something, friends? It seems to me that I can hear people talking in the air, and yet I see no one. Listen!" We were all attentive at his command, and sucked the air into our ears as you would fine oysters on a shell; we strained to hear any sound or voice that might be around. So as not to miss anything, some of us cupped our hands to our ears, as Antoninus the Emperor did.[1] We were forced to admit, nevertheless, that we heard no voices whatsoever.

Pantagruel continued to maintain that he heard various voices in the air, both masculine and feminine. We finally began to think that either we heard them too, or that our ears were ringing. The more intently we listened, the more

---

[7] **baldachins** canopies   [8] **Valfinier** an unidentified person   [9] **hypophetes** one who prophesies past events   [1] He was reputed to have a vast network of secret police

clearly we distinguished the voices; we even began to catch a word or two. This frightened us greatly, and not without cause. We saw no one, and yet we heard voices of men, women, children, and horses. Panurge exclaimed: "Good God, is this a joke? We are lost. Let us flee. There is an ambush for us. Friar John, are you there, my friend? Stay close to me, please. Do you have your sword? Be sure it's not stuck in your scabbard. You don't take enough of the rust off it. We are lost. Listen! By God, those are cannon shots! Let us flee! I don't mean with feet and hands, as Brutus said at the battle of Pharsalia, I mean with sail and oars. Let us flee! I have no courage by sea. In a cellar, or elsewhere, I've enough and more than enough. Let us flee! Let's get out of here! I'm not proposing this out of fear, for I am afraid of nothing save danger. I always say that, and that's what the Archer of Bagnolet[2] used to say. Let's not take any chances of getting our heads cracked. Let us flee. About face. Turn the rudder, son of a whore! Would to God I were now in Quinquenais,[3] even if I never did get married! Let us flee, we are no match for them. There are ten of them to one of us, I swear. And besides, they're on their own manure pile and we're not familiar with the terrain. They will kill us. Let us flee. This is no place for us to be. Demosthenes says that he who flees today lives to fight another day. Let us withdraw, at least. Port, starboard, to the mizzen, hoist the sails, mates. We are dead. Let us flee, by all the devils in hell, let us flee!"

Upon hearing the racket Panurge was making, Pantagruel said: "Who is that coward down there? Let's see first who they are. Maybe they're friends. I still can't see anybody, and I can see a hundred miles around. But listen. I read about a philosopher, Petron[4] by name, who was of the opinion that there were a number of worlds, touching one another and forming an equilateral triangular figure in whose center was the Manor of Truth. Therein dwelled

[2] **Archer of Bagnolet** figures in a famous farce   [3] **Quinquenais** hamlet near Chinon   **Petron,** 6 B.C. Pythagorean philosopher

Words, Ideas, Exemplars, and the Portraits of all things past and future. Around them was the present. In certain years, at great intervals, a portion of these words falls upon humans like catarrhs, or like the dew fell upon Gideon's fleece; the remainder are reserved for the future until the age is fulfilled.

"I also recall that Aristotle maintains that Homer's words are fluttering, flying, moving, and consequently, animated.

"Moreover, Antiphanes said that Plato's doctrine was like words spoken in midwinter which freeze and congeal, without ever being heard. Indeed, children barely understood what Plato taught them, even when they were old men.

"Now is the time to philosophize and to try to find out if, by chance, this could be the spot where such words thaw. How flabbergasted we would be if they came from Orpheus' head and lyre. After the Thracian women tore him to bits, they threw his head and lyre into the river Hebrus;[5] they flowed down the river into the Pontian Sea and floated together to the island of Lesbos. And there came incessantly from his head a lugubrious song, as though it were lamenting Orpheus' death. The lyre, as the wind blew its strings, accompanied the dirge harmoniously. Let us see if we cannot find them here."

How, Among the Thawed Words, Pantagruel Found some Words of Mouth

The pilot answered: "Lord, fear nothing. This is the edge of the Frozen Sea. Here, at the beginning of last winter, there was a great and fierce battle between the Arimaspians[1] and the Nephelibates.[2] The words and cries of men and women froze in the air at that time along with the thud of battle-axes, the clashing of mail and of armor, the neighing of horses, and all the other uproar of battle. Now that winter is over, with the coming of serene and

[5] **Hebrus** river of Thrace that flows into the Aegean [1] **Arimaspians** a Scythian people [2] **Nephelibates** the Cloud-Walkers

temperate weather, this uproar is melting and becoming audible.

"By God," said Panurge, "I believe it. But could we see one of them? I remember reading that, when Moses received the Law of the Jews on the side of the mountain, the people actually saw voices."

"Hold on," said Pantagruel, "look at these! They haven't thawed out yet."

He threw whole handfuls of frozen words on deck, and they looked like striped pills of different colors. We saw words of mouth, green words, blue words, black words, golden words. When we warmed them a bit in our hands, they melted like snow. Then we really heard them! But we were unable to understand them because they were in a barbarous tongue. A rather large one, when warmed in Friar John's hands, popped like chestnuts do when they are thrown on the fire unopened. This made us all jump from fright. "That was the report of a cannon in its day," said Friar John.

Panurge asked Pantagruel to give him some more. Pantagruel said that to give one's word was for lovers. "Sell me some then," said Panurge.

"That's for lawyers," replied Pantagruel. "I'll sell you silence instead, and at a higher price, as Demosthenes sometimes sold it with his *argentangina*." [3]

Nevertheless, Pantagruel threw three or four fistfuls of words on the deck. And I saw some very sharp and bloody words. The pilot said that they returned occasionally to their place of origin only to find that the throat had been slit. I saw horrible words, and others most unpleasant to look at. When they melted we heard: Un, un, un, un, is, tic, torch, lorg, brrdedun, brededac, frr, frrr, frr, bou, bou, bou, bou, bou bou, bou, bou, tracc, tracc, trr, trr, trr, trrr, trrrrr, on, on, on, on, on, ouououououou, goth, magoth, and

---

[3] *argentangina* Demosthenes, bribed by the Milesians not to speak against them, appeared in the Senate with muffled throat and explained that he had *angina* or quinsy. Somebody shouted that he had *argentangina*, *i.e.* money-quinsy

I don't know what other barbaric sounds. And the pilot said that what we heard was the clash of arms and the neighing of horses at the very moment of impact. Then we heard other loud words, which, when they thawed, sounded like drums and fifes, clarions and trumpets. You can believe me when I tell you that this pleased us greatly. I wanted to preserve some words of mouth in oil, as we keep ice and snow between nice clean straw, but Pantagruel was opposed to this. He said that it was senseless to store up something we are never short of. All good and joyous Pantagruelists always have available an abundance of words of mouth.

Then Panurge annoyed Friar John somewhat and made him sulk, for he took him at his word at a time he wasn't expecting it. Friar John threatened to make him repent as Guillaume Jousseaume did when he sold cloth to noble Pathelin, and gave it to him at his word.[4] If Panurge ever married, Friar John vowed to take him by the horns like a calf because Panurge had taken him at his word like a man. Panurge made a face at him in sign of derision, and said: "Would to God I had the word of the Holy Bottle right here and now." [5]

[4] In the *Farce of Pathelin*, the draper sells the lawyer Guillaume Jousseaume his cloth "at his word," and is repaid in kind
[5] the fabulous voyage to the Oracle continues. Its only word will be *Drink*!

SELECTED BIBLIOGRAPHY

Auerbach, Eric, "The World in Pantagruel's Mouth," in *Mimesis,* trans. by Willard Trask. (Princeton, N.J., 1953), pp. 262-84.

Diéguez, Manuel de, *Rabelais par lui-même.* (Paris, 1960).

Febvre, Lucien, *La religion de Rabelais. Le problème de l'incroyance au XVIe siècle.* (Paris, 1947).

Krailsheimer, A. J., *Rabelais and the Franciscans.* (Oxford, 1963).

Lefranc, Abel, *Etudes sur Gargantua, Pantagruel, le Tiers Livre.* (Paris, 1947).

Lewis, D. B. Wyndam, *Doctor Rabelais.* (London and New York, 1957).

Lote, Georges, *La vie et l'oeuvre de François Rabelais.* (Aix-en-Provence, 1938).

Plattard, Jean, *The Life of François Rabelais,* trans. by Louis P. Roche. (New York, 1931).

Putnam, Samuel, *François Rabelais, Man of the Renaissance.* (New York, 1929).

Screech, M. A., *The Rabelaisian Marriage.* (London, 1958).

Spitzer, Leo, "The Works of Rabelais," in *Literary Masterpieces of the Western World,* Francis H. Horn, ed. (Baltimore, 1953), pp. 126-47.

Tilley, Arthur, *François Rabelais.* (Philadelphia and London, 1907).

Willcock, M. P., *The Laughing Philosopher.* (London, 1950).